JUST A LITTLE CHRISTMAS

MERRY FARMER

JUST A LITTLE CHRISTMAS

Copyright ©2020 by Merry Farmer

This book is licensed for your personal enjoyment only. This book may not be re-sold or given away to other people. If you would like to share this book with another person, please purchase an additional copy for each recipient. If you're reading this book and did not purchase it, or it was not purchased for your use only, then please return to your digital retailer and purchase your own copy. Thank you for respecting the hard work of this author.

This book is a work of fiction. Names, characters, places, and incidents are products of the author's imagination or are used fictitiously. Any resemblance to actual events or locales or persons, living or dead, is entirely coincidental.

Cover design by Erin Dameron-Hill (the miracle-worker)

ASIN: B08NHSJWNP

Paperback ISBN: 9798578029547

Click here for a complete list of other works by Merry Farmer.

If you'd like to be the first to learn about when the next books in the series come out and more, please sign up for my newsletter here: http://eepurl.com/RQ-KX

 Created with Vellum

CHAPTER 1

*DARLINGTON GARDENS, EARL'S COURT,
LONDON – DECEMBER, 1890*

Waking up in London was worlds away from waking up in the dozy, Yorkshire countryside. Dawn was only just beginning to break, sending a cold, hazy light through the gap in the curtains covering the window that faced out onto the small park in the middle of the square that was Darlington Gardens. Blake shifted and drew in a deep breath, trying to hold onto sleep for just a few minutes more. It felt like years since he'd slept properly, and he intended to make the most of his newfound contentment.

The source of that blissful contentment slept next to him. With a lazy grin, Blake rolled over and reached for Niall, snuggling against his naked body and sighing happily. It had been six weeks since Blake and Niall, and Blake's two daughters, Greta and Jessie, had moved to London and taken up residence in one of the townhouses in Darlington Gardens, but Blake still felt as though the simple act of nestling his naked body against Niall's as the two of them slept, not a soul in the world caring that the two of them were together, and the vast majority of the people who knew Blake not even aware of where he was or what he was doing, was a miracle.

Things were still far from perfect. Blake's soon-to-be ex-wife, Annamarie, was missing somewhere in England and she had his son and heir to the Selby dukedom, Alan, with her. But John Dandie had every resource at his disposal invested in locating them and Annamarie's lover, Ian Archibald, a former university classmate of Blake's and Niall's, who was likely responsible for what amounted to kidnapping and extortion. The gnawing restlessness of being separated from his son was a constant presence in Blake's mind, but it was matched and countered by the absolute joy of being together with Niall again in every way that mattered and having his daughters with them.

Blake was well on his way to falling back into sleep, an arm and leg thrown over Niall, generating even more warmth under the copious layers of blankets covering them in the frosty room. The fire had gone out at some point during the night—something that had been happening frequently, since Blake's valet, Xavier, was the only servant they'd hired to tend the house so far—but the cold snap in the room only made snuggling with Niall that much more enjoyable.

Outside, even though it was still mostly dark, the square was already coming to life. Horses clopped along the paved street, likely drawing wagons delivering everything from coal to meat to the houses that made up Darlington Gardens. The dog that Stephen Siddel had let the girls of his orphanage—two doors down from Blake and Niall's home—adopt barked at something. The quiet voices of servants from the other houses and tradesmen bartering just barely filtered through the more distant sound of traffic from the major road that ran parallel to the other side of the square. Even at dawn, the city was filled with sound and people. Blake had spent most of his life in the quiet country, but for the first time, even with the racket, he felt like he was home.

Awareness of the buzzing city banished his last hope of sleeping in, so he turned his focus to Niall. His adored lover was still asleep, his chest rising and falling steadily as he lay on his back. Blake grinned against Niall's bare shoulder and raked his fingers through the light hair on his chest, feeling Niall's heartbeat. His grin widened and he kissed and nipped Niall's shoulder as he moved his hand to tease Niall's nipple, then ventured slowly downward across the firm, flat plane of Niall's belly. When he reached Niall's already half-erect cock and stroked down to grasp his balls, Niall sucked in a breath, waking.

Blake couldn't repress his laughter as Niall tensed and blinked before turning his head to stare blearily at him. "Are you fondling me in my sleep?" he asked in a slurred, barely awake voice.

"No," Blake teased him. "Because you're awake now. Very awake." He proved his point by stroking Niall more enthusiastically, taking special care to stimulate the flared tip of Niall's prick with a light touch.

Niall groaned in a way Blake suspected was meant to convey mock disapproval, but ended up proving just how much Niall liked to be awakened that way, and stretched. He twisted his arm that was trapped between the two of them, seeking out Blake's own morning erection to return the favor. Blake helped him along by shifting so that Niall could handle him fully, then let out a sigh of deep approval at the sensation. That wasn't quite enough on its own, so he rocked into Niall's touch, sighing louder as he did.

At least until Niall laughed, "You're incorrigible."

Blake paused his stroking to lift himself on one arm and grin down at Niall. The man was gorgeous first thing in the morning, hair tousled, eyes puffy from sleep, utterly relaxed. "You like me this way," he said, scooting closer and brushing his hand over Niall's chest and side for a moment before resuming his attention on his cock.

"What way?" Niall continued to laugh, affection, contentment, and pleasure sparkling in his blue eyes.

"Insatiable," Blake murmured, dipping closer and stealing a kiss from Niall's warm lips. "Oversexed." He nudged his way between Niall's legs and balanced over top of him, kissing him longer and harder. "Ready for it all the time." He kissed Niall a third time, arching his hips so that their cocks rubbed together.

Niall gasped, then moaned at the contact, gripping Blake's sides under the covers. "God, do I ever," he groaned before another passionate kiss from Blake drowned out anything else he might have said.

It was pure, undiluted, perfection. Blake made no apologies for being hungry for it all the time after ten years without a shred of real pleasure or love. Niall was the love of his life, and fate and circumstance had kept them apart for far too long. All that was over now, and he intended to enjoy his lover to the fullest as often as he possibly could. He reached between them, grasping both of their pricks together and jerking in a way designed to bring them both to quick and satisfying orgasms.

He was well on his way to achieving that goal—and could tell from the tension in his body that Niall was too—when the bedroom door creaked open, letting in a burst of light.

"Papa, I've just had a horrible thought," seven-year-old Jessie said in a small, bleary morning voice from the doorway.

Blake and Niall both went rigid with shock and embarrassment, and a dozen other emotions that Blake was sure he would never recover from. He thanked God for thick bedcovers and a room that was dark, but there was no way at all to hide his and Niall's bare shoulders, or the fact that Blake was clearly on top of Niall and their mouths had been locked together when Jessie saw them.

MERRY FARMER

"Darling, what are you doing out of bed so early?" Blake managed to say in a shaky voice.

He did his best to wriggle off of Niall and to face Jessie, but in his current condition, there was no possible way he could throw back the bedcovers or get out of bed. Since Niall couldn't possibly have gotten away either, the best he could do was to rest on his side behind Blake, holding his breath as though he was waiting to see just how dire the situation was.

"I had a bad thought," Jessie said, making her way to the bed as though she intended to climb in with Blake, the way she always had when they lived at Selby Manor in Yorkshire. She was wrapped in a thick robe, her hair a tangled mess, and her eyes droopy, as though she wasn't fully awake. Blake had a moment of serious, erection-withering panic as Jessie reached the bed, but fortunately, she stopped before getting in. Worry clouded her sweet, young face as she asked, "What if Father Christmas doesn't know where to find us this year?"

Blake swallowed hard, glancing over his shoulder at Niall. Surely, Jessie must have seen him there. Niall wasn't exactly hiding under the covers, and even if he had been, Jessie had most certainly walked in on them entwined. He shifted back to Jessie, reaching out a hand to stroke her head, and said, "Sweetheart, Father Christmas knows where we are now."

"Are you certain?" Jessie narrowed her eyes, looking a bit more awake, and bit her lip.

"Yes, dear. He's Father Christmas, after all," Blake told her.

"But we moved to London so quickly," Jessie went on. "He might not have had time to update his list."

A thread of suspicion had Blake raising one eyebrow. "Did someone tell you Father Christmas wouldn't be able to find you this year?"

Jessie nodded and said, "Ursula said Father Christmas is very busy this time of year."

"Ursula from Stephen's orphanage?" Niall asked, peering over Blake's bare shoulder at Jessie.

Jessie's gaze shifted to him and she nodded. Nothing at all in her expression or her stance indicated she thought it was unusual for Niall to be in bed with her papa. "She said it could take him years to update his list."

"No, sweetheart, Ursula is wrong." Blake scooted forward as much as he dared so that he could kiss Jessie's cheek awkwardly. "I promise you that Father Christmas will find us this year. You'll see. Now go back to bed, and I'll be up to help you get dressed in a bit."

"Yes, Papa." Jessie smiled and leaned forward to kiss Blake's cheek, then skipped back to the doorway. At the last minute, she turned to ask, "Papa, why aren't you and Niall wearing night shirts? It's cold."

Blake's mouth fell open, and he stammered and stuttered, no idea how to come up with an explanation.

"We have too many blankets on the bed, so we took them off because we got hot," Niall offered.

"Oh." Jessie said, blinked, then shrugged and continued on her way.

"Darling, shut the door behind you," Blake called after her.

Jessie skipped back to shut the door—a little too loudly. As soon as she did, Blake let out a heavy breath and collapsed to his side. Niall, on the other hand, had the audacity to laugh as he tumbled to his back and covered his face with his hands.

"It's not funny," Blake scolded him, shifting to his side and glaring at Niall. "I think my soul left my body the moment she threw open the door."

"Why doesn't the door have a lock again?" Niall asked, still laughing, his face red in the dim light.

"I'll be getting one immediately," Blake said, sliding out of bed and crossing to flick the switch that turned on the brand-new electric lights that illuminated the room. All of the houses being built in Earl's Court, whether they were in Darlington Gardens and part of The Brotherhood's enclave or not, had been built with the very latest in electrical and plumbing technology. Blake felt as though he were living in a modern marvel, but it still hadn't been enough to keep his daughter from walking in on him at the most delicate moment possible.

"How on earth are we going to explain to Jessie what she saw?" he asked as he walked into the washroom that had been built adjacent to the bedroom. He turned on the sink and splashed ice-cold water over his face.

A moment later, Niall was in the washroom with

JUST A LITTLE CHRISTMAS

him, embracing him from behind and pressing the erection he still had against Blake's backside. "I'm not sure we'll have to explain anything. I don't think she had the slightest clue what she was looking at, and in my experience, the less said to the ignorant the better." He glanced at the picture the two of them made in the mirror that hung above the sink and said to Blake's reflection. "Any interest in finishing what we started?"

Blake laughed ironically, even though the sight of Niall's arms around him, their heads close together and their mouths still pink from kisses, warmed him in ways he couldn't begin to express. "Not until we invest in a lock," he said. "Jessie might come back and bring Greta with her."

Niall laughed low in his throat, kissed the side of Blake's neck lingeringly, then stepped away, smacking Blake's bare backside as he did. "I'll purchase a lock the moment the stores open," he said before heading back into the bedroom.

Blake watched him go, joy filling his heart in spite of the fright they'd had. After a decade of wandering in the proverbial wilderness, how was it possible for him to be so happy? Was it right for him to feel such a sense of love and rightness when Alan was still in Annamarie and Ian's hands?

That thought sobered him a bit and helped him focus on his morning toilet, dressing, and making his way downstairs to see if the cook they'd hired had breakfast ready. He had full faith in John Dandie and his contacts to locate Alan and return him. John had already initiated divorce proceedings on his behalf, so as soon as Anna-marie was located, all she would have to do was sign a piece of paper and they would both be free. He and the girls would stay hidden in Earl's Court in the meantime, which suited him just fine. In spite of being a duke, Blake had discovered he rather liked the life of a middle-class housewife.

"Girls, we need to have a frank discussion about privacy," he said with a serious look once all five of them —him and Blake, Greta, Jessie, and Xavier—were all seated at the breakfast table, enjoying ham, eggs, toast, and tea. "Situations have changed, and you cannot simply leap into my bed whenever you have a nightmare or a bad thought, as you did before." His face burned red as he glanced from his right hand, where Greta sat, to his left, were Jessie watched him with an innocent smile.

"Is that because Niall sleeps in your bed now, Papa?" Greta asked, sipping her tea as though she were asking if it was going to snow in time for Christmas.

Xavier dropped his fork against his plate—the poor man still wasn't used to being treated like a member of the family instead of a servant, no matter how many reas-surances Blake made to him, nor was he used to such frank talk—and Niall snorted as though he'd tried to hold back a laugh.

Blake opted for simple honesty and prayed he wouldn't have to explain. "Yes, it is."

Greta and Jessie exchanged a look across the table

that made Blake wonder if the two had had a wager of some sort, and if so, which of them had won.

Greta finished her sip of tea, set her cup down, picked up her toast, and casually said, "Mr. Siddel and Max sleep in the same bed as well."

Xavier dropped his fork a second time, his face going beet red as he coughed.

"Is that so?" Niall asked, seemingly nonplussed.

"Yes," Jessie said. "That's what Jane told me."

Blake opened his mouth, on the verge of asking Jessie what she thought about the arrangement, but when Niall shook his head slightly, he changed tack. "You girls don't mind doing your lessons with the girls at the orphanage, do you? We need to hire a maid, and I was thinking of hiring a governess as well, but—"

"No! I don't want a governess!"

"I love doing lessons at the orphanage!"

The rush of protest from the girls was enough to banish the idea of a governess from Blake's mind. In truth, he was glad to have one less thing to worry about and one fewer person who might alert the rest of the world to where his odd family was.

"That's settled, then," he said. Everyone else at the table was treating the meal and the conversation as if they were perfectly normal—except perhaps Xavier, who looked as stunned as if he'd fallen through the looking glass—so he went on as though nothing were out of the ordinary. "When Niall and I drop you off at the orphanage after breakfast before we run our errands—"

which involved checking in with John about the latest developments in the search for Annamarie, paying a call to his bank about freezing more of the assets Annamarie was attempting to get her hands on, and dropping by the Concord Theater so Niall could check on the latest box office take of his current play, "—we'll ask Mr. Siddel if he requires any further sort of payment to educate you little minxes."

The girls giggled and continued with their breakfast. Blake shot a look to Niall to see what he thought. It was mad of him to think so, but ever since he and Niall had committed to living out the rest of their lives as one, Blake felt the need to clear any financial decision with Niall, even though his money was technically his own.

"I think that sounds like a brilliant idea," Niall said with a saucy wink. Blake had the feeling Niall rather enjoyed being the king of their particular castle.

Half an hour later, as their cook cleared away the breakfast table and Xavier headed upstairs to carry out the duties of an upstairs maid—not that he minded, or so he swore, since it gave him the opportunity to live on such a fascinating square with so many attractive neighbors—Blake and Niall stepped into the cheerful chaos of the Darlington Gardens Orphanage.

Breakfast was just finishing up for the dozens of girls who called the unusual establishment their home. The dining room, with its numerous, round tables—so very different from the long, stodgy tables of every other institution Blake had ever known—was brightly lit and deco-

JUST A LITTLE CHRISTMAS

rated with flowers and murals of bucolic scenes. In fact, a gentleman that Niall had informed Blake was a renowned set painter was hard at work on one side of the room, adding a startlingly life-like tiger to the painted menagerie already on the wall. Several other gentlemen from the square were on hand as well, helping to clear places or tutor the girls before lessons, or brushing and styling their hair. One or two of them wore dresses as pretty as the orphans' uniforms and cosmetics to match.

"Sometimes I feel as though we've stepped right out of reality and into a storybook," Blake whispered to Niall —uncertain if the fact made him happy or just shocked him—as Stephen Siddel waved to them from the head table at the front of the room.

"Didn't I tell you that Shakespeare was right and that there are more things on heaven and earth than are dreamed of in your philosophy?" Niall whispered back to him as Greta and Jessie broke away to join their friends, Jane and Katie, at a nearby table.

Blake laughed and shook his head. "I've no idea what the rest of the world would think if they knew about this place."

"They would deny it." Niall nodded to Stephen as he joined them. "And History will forget it happened entirely, if that is what future generations deem convenient," he added with an arch of one eyebrow.

"Your grace," Stephen greeted Blake, shaking his hand, then shook Niall's as well.

"For the love of God, please don't call me that here,"

MERRY FARMER

Blake laughed. "As far as Darlington Gardens is concerned, I'm Mr. Williamson."

"You'd better heed him," Niall said with mock seriousness. "A duke gets what a duke wants, after all."

Blake sent him a flat, sideways look and shook his head.

Stephen seemed amused by the exchange, but from everything Blake knew of the man so far, Stephen Siddel was the sort of contented soul who found joy and amusement in everything. "Is there something I can do for you this morning, gentlemen?" he asked.

"We just came to ask about tuition fees for Greta and Jessie, since they're determined to see your establishment as their school," Blake said.

"And while we're at it," Niall added with a sly grin, before Stephen could answer, "do you have any advice for keeping overly curious girls from walking in on things they shouldn't see first thing in the morning?"

Blake's face went hot at the question, and he was tempted to jab his elbow into Niall's side.

"Locks," Maxwell Hillsboro answered, walking into the room as the last of the girls hurried out for their lessons. "Plenty of locks." He headed straight to Stephen's side, stealing a quick kiss from Stephen's lips and taking his hand with a wink. "And a strict set of rules about quiet time and community time."

Stephen looked as sheepish as Blake felt and grinned. "I second the locks," he said. "It's quite a balancing act, maintaining the roles of father and partner."

JUST A LITTLE CHRISTMAS

"I'll say it is." Niall grinned.

Blake shook his head slowly. The conversation was as incongruous to everything he'd always believed was normal and ordinary as the men in drag helping out at the orphanage. Niall had told him before they'd moved that London had far more layers than the country, and that some of those layers were astoundingly open to their sort. He hadn't truly believed it until living there, though.

"Speaking of fathers," Niall said, sending a pointed glance to Stephen. "One of your girls told Jessie that Father Christmas wouldn't be able to find her or Greta here this year because of the move."

Max rolled his eyes. Stephen sighed and asked, "Which one?"

"Ursula?" Blake thought he remembered the name.

"I'll tell her that's nonsense," Max said.

"But it brings up another thought," Niall went on. "Have you made any sort of plans yet for Christmas festivities for the orphans and the rest of the children living in the square?"

The question had Blake smiling from ear to ear in an instant. Niall had become a sort of father figure to his girls practically overnight. Blake had always known he would be a good father, and Niall had professed to like children, but hearing him express such sentimental and caring concerns warmed Blake's heart in ways he couldn't have imagined.

"We've barely had time to breathe, let alone plan Christmas festivities," Stephen said with a self-deprecating laugh, shoving a hand through his hair and knocking his glasses askew as he did. "Did you have any ideas?"

Niall grinned modestly. "You're talking to a famous playwright. Of course, I have ideas for a Christmas pantomime that we could stage for the girls. I thought we could take the story of—"

Niall didn't have a chance to finish. Out in the hallway, the front door banged open. A rush of cold air sped down the hall, along with a pink-faced, wide-eyed girl in one of the orphanage's newly designed uniforms.

"Sir! Sir!" she shouted as Stephen and Max dashed into the hall, Blake and Niall following. "There's a policeman in the square!"

CHAPTER 2

*D*arlington Gardens was a paradise, as far as Stephen was concerned. A paradise that he couldn't have imagined last Christmas. The square had only just been finished a year before. The large, rectangular neighborhood of terraced flats and townhouses that surrounded a gated park filled with trees, garden beds, and play areas for children was the brain child of Danny Long, pub owner, property developer, and one of the wealthiest men in London. He'd named the square after his wife, the former Lady Phoebe Darlington, whom he adored, and had sold, leased, or rented every building in the place to members of The Brotherhood.

But not only was Darlington Gardens a safe and secret enclave for men who wished to live as they pleased with other men—and a few women with the women they loved—it was the new home of the orphanage Stephen

MERRY FARMER

had spent the greater part of his adult life running. He'd feared the worst for his girls after the previous building housing the orphanage on Briar Street in Limehouse had been burnt to the ground in an act of vengeance by his lover and partner Max's father, Lord Eastleigh, but The Brotherhood had stepped up and pitched in to allow Stephen to lease the enormous building complex that made up the orphanage from Danny. Best of all, the nature of Darlington Gardens made it possible for Stephen and Max to live and love openly together, though neither they nor any of the other men who made the square their home dared to behave the way they could inside the square when they stepped so much as three inches outside of the neighborhood.

Which was why news that a policeman had arrived in the square was an event worthy of panic.

"Did he say what he wanted?" Stephen asked Beatrice as she led him and Max, with Niall and Blake trailing them, out of the warm and comfortable orphanage and into the freezing street.

"No, sir," Beatrice said, hugging herself as she kept up to his side. "He's just nosing."

That alone was reason to be concerned. The last thing any of the residents of Darlington Gardens needed was nosing. Just the week before, there had been a raid on a much smaller neighborhood in Marylebone that was home to several men Stephen knew. Some obnoxious and spiteful blackmailer had drawn one of the residents into a tryst that was designed to expose the poor idiot and lead

18

JUST A LITTLE CHRISTMAS

to his arrest. Blackmailers like that were an increasing problem for men like them since the Cleveland Street scandal the year before. The scandal involved the exposure of a male brothel whose clientele was made up of prominent men, many of them members of the nobility. It was rumored that the Prince of Wales himself and at least one royal duke patronized the place, but of course none of their names had appeared in the papers that were so eagerly devoured throughout the subsequent trial. The whole scandal had been extraordinarily sordid, but the public had eaten it up and was hungry for more, similar stories. Which was why Darlington Gardens was such a haven.

It was still early morning, but the sun had risen just enough to peek over the tops of the buildings on the east side of the square. The frost of the night before had burnt off in the sunny patches, but it still covered the limbs of the trees in the park and the doorsteps and windowsills on the shady side of the square. Several tradesmen had their wagons parked along the street—though there would be even more in the mews that ringed the square on the other side of the buildings—and a surprisingly large number of people were out and about in the chilly morning. Though, the closer Stephen looked, the more he could see that several of those men milling about were keeping a sharp eye on the uniformed officer peering over the low wall around the park and squinting into the bushes, as though he would find something salacious there. The lout would be sorely disappointed to know the

MERRY FARMER

park was enjoyed mostly by children at play and not men in search of illicit entertainment, like so many other parks throughout the city. That was what made Darlington Gardens unique.

"Do we approach him to ask what he's doing here?" Max asked, jogging up to Stephen's side. He carried Stephen's thick, winter coat—which Stephen hadn't bothered to take from its peg near the door in his haste to see what was going on—and held it up so that he could shrug into it.

"If he's anything like the coppers who loiter around the theater," Niall said, "we should leave him alone. He's sniffing for trouble, and we don't want to give it to him."

"I should say not," Blake agreed.

Stephen rubbed his chin and adjusted his glasses, which had fogged up momentarily in the shift from warm to cold. He glanced up and down the street on their side of the square for a reason the four of them would be loitering in the early morning. As luck would have it, a very good reason to be out presented itself immediately.

"I didn't know David and Lionel were moving in today," he said, nodding to the wagon of furniture that was being unloaded in front of one of the townhouses near the narrow northeastern entrance to the square. "Let's welcome them home."

Max grinned and nodded, as though he could see what Stephen had in mind, and the four of them ambled casually to the northeast corner of the square. Danny had designed the square to be almost entirely self-contained.

JUST A LITTLE CHRISTMAS

It had only two, narrow entrances—one in the northeast corner and one in the northwest corner—each little more than a single lane wide enough to let a wagon as large as the one bringing in Lionel and David's furniture to pass. Many of the other squares that were being built in Earl's Court in such a way as to imitate the grander neighborhoods of Mayfair, like Grosvenor Square and Berkeley Square, were constructed with a similar design, but the thoroughfares leading in and out of Darlington Gardens were narrower on purpose to keep residents as isolated as possible.

"So the two of you are finally darkening our doorsteps, are you?" Max asked in a jovial voice as their group approached the stairs leading up to David and Lionel's new house.

Lionel stood at the top of the stairs, directing the removers like a conductor in front of an orchestra while David lent a hand, hauling a crate of books from the back of the wagon and carrying it into the house.

"This is the newest fashionable address in London," Lionel explained with a shrug, his high voice deceptively light. He might have looked like a dandy to the point that even a blind man could peg him as a homosexual from half a mile away, but Lionel Mercer was one of the cleverest and most deadly men Stephen knew. "How could we not move here?" Lionel finished with a sly wink.

"I would have been fine to continue on in my comfortable, well-appointed, completely paid-for house,"

David said with a grunt as he passed them with his crate of books. "But someone wanted to have more of a social life."

"You're just as social a creature as I am," Lionel called after him once David disappeared inside. "And you enjoy spending time with Stephen's girls as much as anyone else does."

"Mr. Wirth is ever so smart," Beatrice added with a fond grin. Stephen raised his eyebrows. He hadn't noticed her coming after them down the street. Then again, it was Beatrice's ability to go unobserved that had alerted them to the potential problem in their midst in the first place.

"It's a grand place to live," Stephen agreed, pivoting slightly so that he stood by Lionel's side, facing the corner of the street where the police officer had moved in order to peer into the park more deeply. "It's safe and undisturbed."

Max moved to stand by Stephen's side, and Niall and Blake pretended to be interested in the contents of the remover's wagon so that they could all watch the officer.

Lionel hummed and tapped a finger to his pink lips, which stood out against his pale, cold-kissed complexion. "We noticed the welcoming committee as soon as we arrived."

Stephen's pulse kicked up in alarm. "How long has he been here?" he said in a serious voice, leaning closer to Lionel.

JUST A LITTLE CHRISTMAS

"At least half an hour," Lionel murmured in return. "I don't think it's a mystery what he's looking for."

"He's not going to find it," Max said, more out of determination to keep the man in the dark than because there was anything to find. They all knew full well there was plenty that a greedy officer intent on making a name for himself by exposing what too much of the rest of the world would have seen as a viper's den could find.

"How do we get rid of him?" Stephen asked.

"Does anyone have some dogs they could sic on the lout?" Lionel asked in return.

Stephen huffed a laugh. "We have one mangy mutt who would be more likely to lick the man to death than frighten him away."

There was a pause as they watched the officer come around the corner of the park. The man noticed them all staring, though everyone did their best to look otherwise occupied as soon as he narrowed his eyes at them. Niall and Blake fell into conversation with Beatrice while several of the gents loitering on their front stoops stepped back into their houses.

"Should someone fetch Danny Long?" Max asked as the officer began to walk toward them more deliberately. Danny and Phoebe had moved into the house at the far end of the square that bordered Earls Court Road. The building ran the entire length of that end of the square—which Lady Phoebe said was a hundred times more space than the two of them needed, even with their growing family—but the palatial home served

MERRY FARMER

as the most effective buffer to the rest of the world that any of the Darlington Gardens residents could have asked for.

Lionel scoffed at the idea. "We don't need Mr. Long to solve our problems for us." He stepped forward just as the officer reached the remover's wagon. "Good morning, Officer. What a relief to be welcomed to our new home by such a valiant protector as you."

Stephen eyed Lionel warily as he stepped down from his front stoop and extended a kid-gloved hand to the man. Lionel might have been one of the most powerful men in London, but his methods were a little too overt for Stephen's comfort.

The officer seemed to think so as well. He narrowed his eyes at Lionel instead of taking his hand. "Who are you, sir, when you're at home?" he demanded.

"Lionel Mercer, at your service." Lionel withdrew his hand as though the officer had given him a hearty hand-shake. "And you are?"

"Officer Murdoch." The man tilted his nose up, failing to hide a sneer as he glanced from Lionel to Stephen and Max. He seemed to ignore Niall and Blake, clearly having no idea they were one of London's most celebrated playwrights and a duke. "I was told something fishy was going on around here."

Stephen arched an eyebrow, working to maintain an outward calm while his heart raced. "Something fishy, sir?" He shrugged and glanced to Max as if asking whether Max had a clue what that meant.

24

JUST A LITTLE CHRISTMAS

"You know." Officer Murdoch sniffed and went on. "Strange things."

"I cannot possibly imagine what you mean," Lionel said with an affable smile.

Stephen figured he was counting on Officer Murdoch's squeamishness to shut the man down. As often as not, any man who admitted to knowing about the character of a neighborhood such as theirs ran the risk of being implicated by association. That, along with ignorance and innocence, was one of the most effective safety precautions their lot had.

"I'm sure he means the shenanigans our girls get up to," Stephen laughed, taking a risk and drawing the officer's attention. He held out a hand. "Stephen Siddel," he introduced himself. "Proprietor of the Darlington Gardens Orphanage, which is just over there, number nine." He nodded to the orphanage.

Officer Murdoch shook his hand, which was a good sign. "There's an orphanage on this square?" he asked.

"Yes," Stephen answered. "An orphanage for girls. We are home to nearly thirty sweet young souls at the moment." He glanced to Max, then added, "This is my co-proprietor, Mr. Maxwell Hillsboro." Max had long since given up calling himself by his noble title or having anything at all to do with his former life.

"I see." Officer Murdoch shook Max's hand as well, another promising sign. "You gents wouldn't have seen any...inappropriate behavior hereabouts, would you?" he asked.

"No, nothing," Max said with a baffled look and a shake of his head. Which was a blatant lie, if one considered he'd been enraptured by the sight of Stephen sucking him off in the pre-dawn hours that morning. When Max peeked in his direction, Stephen had to force himself to look away, lest he give away his true feelings.

Officer Murdoch narrowed his eyes as though he suspected something. "It's just that I've had reports," he said.

"From whom?" Stephen asked.

Officer Murdoch rolled his shoulders and sniffed. "People."

It was all Stephen could do not to roll his eyes. The man was going to be a bigger problem than they needed.

"How might we contact you if and when we notice anything amiss?" he asked, pretending to be deeply concerned.

"Send for me from Scotland Yard," the man said, full of self-importance. "Ask for Officer Richard Murdoch."

"We will," Max told the man with a smile.

Officer Murdoch nodded, then touched the brim of his hat and walked on.

"Tell me about the furnishings again." Stephen pretended to start a conversation with Lionel as they all watched the man leave the square by the northeast entrance.

"They cost a fortune, of course," Lionel played along.

Somehow, they managed to keep up the banter until they were certain Officer Murdoch truly was gone. About

JUST A LITTLE CHRISTMAS

that same time, David walked out of the house with a scowl.

"I saw him head off down the street from the library window," he growled, then added a curse under his breath.

"What's the point of having a safe neighborhood if policemen think they can corner us like fish in a barrel?" Niall asked, rejoining the conversation.

"Barrels don't have corners, darling," Blake told him with a besotted grin.

"Don't you start with me." Niall pretended to be at his wit's end with Blake, though if Stephen knew anything about the sort of looks the two were darting at each other, they'd be tangled up, doing exactly the sort of thing Officer Murdoch was on the hunt for, within fifteen minutes.

"We should send word to Lord Clerkenwell," Max said, infinitely more serious. "He would be able to quell whatever curiosity this Officer Murdoch has."

"Must we always go running to daddy for help whenever we find ourselves in a bind?" Lionel huffed. "I like Jack Craig as much as the next man—and what a shame it is that he is so devoted to his wife and family—but it irks me to wring my hands and seek the help of the Assistant Commissioner every time we have a scare. Even if the man is friendly to our cause."

"I agree with Lionel," David said. "This situation doesn't warrant bothering Lord Clerkenwell yet. We can handle things on our own."

MERRY FARMER

"Agreed," Stephen said with a hesitant sigh, though something in him felt as though the problem might end up bigger than they could handle on their own, if they weren't careful. "We'll get the word out to everyone else and form a watch committee." He hesitated, then turned to Niall and said, "Perhaps we shouldn't go on with the idea of a Christmas pantomime for the girls with this threat hanging over our heads."

"A Christmas panto?" Lionel interrupted before Niall could protest, lighting up like a string of electric lights. "That's a wonderful idea."

"Is it?" David frowned and crossed his arms, as though he wasn't so sure. "Christmas pantomimes are infamous for their *frivolity*." He spoke the word carefully, though they all knew he meant men in drag and gender-bending silliness. "Is that really the kind of attention we want to be drawing at the moment?"

"My girls are worried Father Christmas won't visit them this year," Blake said with a protective vehemence Stephen found endearing. "It's been a trying year for everyone."

"Which is why I believe a small, private pantomime, performed somewhere in the neighborhood, would be exactly the sort of festivity everyone needs this year," Niall finished the thought.

"We could do it discreetly," Stephen agreed. "To be honest, the more I consider the idea, the more I would like to make this year's Christmas celebration as delightful for the girls as possible. Several of the poor

JUST A LITTLE CHRISTMAS

souls living under my roof now were victims of the kidnapping ring last Christmas. They need something jolly to show them life is good after all and no one will harm them here."

That seemed to be the deciding factor. Even David loosened his perpetual frown to agree that merriment was needed.

"If you're going to stage anything, Everett will want to play the lead," Lionel said as the energy shifted and their group brightened at the idea of a show.

"Everett wouldn't be Everett if he didn't demand to play the lead," Niall agreed. "He's still staring nightly in *Love's Last Lesson*, though, and we've added performances for the Christmas season."

"He has an understudy, doesn't he?" Lionel asked. "I'm certain whoever that is would relish the chance to take the role for a night, just as I'm positive Everett would be far more interested in performing for the orphans than a crowd of priggish theatergoers any day."

"Are you joking?" David laughed. "Everett is more likely to want to perform the panto in the afternoon, then rush to the theater to dazzle those prigs in the evening."

"We could always ask which he'd rather do," Max said with a shrug.

"An excellent idea," Lionel said, clapping his hands together. "I'll go to his flat this very minute to ask him." He took a few steps away from them.

"Lionel, wait," David called after him. "We're in the

middle of moving. You need to help me carry boxes and furniture inside and arrange everything."

"What was that?" Lionel feigned innocence, cupping a hand to his ear, though he was only ten feet away. "I can't hear you. Time is wasting. I have to reach Everett before he secures another engagement."

David shook his head—though he grinned as he did, especially when Lionel blew him a kiss before disappearing around the corner—and sighed. "Unbelievable."

"You knew there was no way he would risk getting his gloves dirty by helping unload the wagon anyhow," Max said with a laugh, thumping David's shoulder. "We'll help."

"We most certainly will," Stephen said, following Max to the wagon with the others. "Because that's what we do in Darlington Gardens. We help each other."

And they'd made the square their own bit of heaven by doing it.

CHAPTER 3

*E*verett Jewel woke with a start, his heart racing, panic making his fingers numb and his head spin. He spent a moment thrashing against his sheets, fighting the ghostly force that had menaced him in yet another nightmare. But unlike every other time he'd had the same nightmare in the past, as soon as he knew he was awake, calm rushed over him. He twisted onto his back and relaxed, breathing as steadily as he could until it wasn't an effort anymore and rubbing a hand over his sweaty face. It came away with just a bit of stage make-up, which he apparently hadn't scrubbed off all the way from the previous night's performance of *Love's Last Lesson*. He didn't mind a bit of lingering make-up if Patrick didn't mind.

Patrick. His heart warmed and steadied even more, and he reached across the bed for the man who had given his life meaning and who kept him grounded. But the bed

MERRY FARMER

beside him was empty. He felt up and down the sheets just to be sure, as if he'd missed something, then opened his eyes and turned his head.

"Patrick?" he called out, sitting abruptly, panic gripping him again. Their bedroom was empty and the only clothes strewn across the chair in the corner from the night before were his own. "Patrick?" he shouted again, swinging his legs over the side of the bed, ready to race to the ends of the earth to get his lover back if he had to.

"Where's the fire?" Patrick asked, stepping into the bedroom doorway. He wore an apron over his plain shirt and trousers and a teasing grin as he took in the sight of Everett's naked body.

Everett let out a sigh of relief and rubbed a hand over his face, cursing himself for being a worrying ninny. Of course Patrick hadn't gone anywhere or left him. He should have noted the details of their flat before he shot straight to panic. The fire in their bedroom crackled merrily. The scent of bacon and coffee wafted from the main room. The curtains had been open to let in crisp, morning sunlight. And only his clothes from the day before were lying out because Patrick was meticulously tidy, had already cleaned up after himself, but was trying to make a point about how slovenly Everett was by refusing to pick up after him.

"There is no fire," Everett said sheepishly, flopping back onto the bed, arms spread, legs dangling over the side. "As usual, I'm being dramatic." He added a sigh for effect, though the real emotion that coursed through him

JUST A LITTLE CHRISTMAS

as Patrick stepped deeper into the room was bone-deep relief. His past was behind him. Chisolm couldn't hurt him anymore. The man dead, and as unnerving as the ghost of him making appearances in Everett's dreams was, it was powerless. He was safe and happy, adored in his role in Niall's play, and genuinely loved by Patrick.

"Nightmares again?" Patrick asked, walking over to the bed and standing between Everett's knees, his arms crossed.

Everett arched one eyebrow as he looked up at him, his prick jumping to life. "I don't think they're ever truly going to go away," he admitted, serious in spite of the swirl of desire and impishness pulsing through him. It was fully within his character to be both deadly serious about the darker side of life and randy as a satyr simultaneously, and the sight of Patrick's large, powerful body looming over him never failed to arouse him.

Patrick glanced down at Everett's growing erection with a devilish grin, arms still crossed. "You know what we say to nightmares, don't you?" he asked, sinking to his knees and resting his large hands on Everett's thighs, pushing them wider.

Everett sucked in a breath of anticipation and propped himself on his elbows to have a better view. "We say we're not home to Mr. Nightmare," he repeated the silly line Patrick had insisted he recite every time he woke in a sweat in the middle of the night. Of course, as often as not, if he was in a sweat in the middle of the night, it was for an entirely different reason.

33

MERRY FARMER

He let out a long, impassioned moan a moment later as Patrick took his prick in hand and stroked it until he was fully hard. It didn't matter how long the two of them had been together or how many times Patrick had touched him exactly as he was now, it felt as intensely pleasurable as if he were being handled for the first time. Patrick's wry grin was as commanding as if he'd ordered Everett to commit every sort of act of depravity and left Everett feeling just as much like putty in his hands—or rather, in his mouth as he leaned in to swallow him.

"Have I mentioned yet today how much I love you?" Everett gasped as Patrick worked on him, taking him deep and doing the thing with his tongue that God only knew where he'd learned it, but thank the same God he had. The wet heat of Patrick's mouth, the friction and sucking, and the way Patrick had enough presence of mind and dexterity to tease his balls and finger his hole while moving deftly on him had Everett right at the edge in the blink of an eye. "Oh, fuck," he growled, coming so suddenly it was almost embarrassing.

Patrick swallowed reflexively, then leaned back, catching his breath and wiping his mouth with the back of his hand—all of which Everett found impossibly endearing and sensual. "*That* is what we say to night-mares," he panted, mirth glittering in his eyes. He stood, pulling the apron off over his head and revealing an impressive bulge in his trousers. "Now roll over and spread that fine arse for me, because I'm not finished yet."

Everett made a sound between a laugh and a

whimper as Patrick undid his trousers and stepped to the bedside table to unscrew the lid of the ointment they kept there. He did as he was ordered and shifted to his stomach, holding his arse up and practically shaking with anticipation. There he was, Everett Jewel, darling of the London stage—men and women throwing themselves at him on a nightly basis, commanding crowds and shining like the fiery star he was—shouting every sort of delicious obscenity he could think of as the man he adored with his whole heart slammed his thick hard cock up his arse.

He really did love everything about the way Patrick fucked him, from the bruising way Patrick gripped his hips as he thrust mercilessly, to the sensation of being stretched and pounded, to the soul-piercing trust and surrender that came with the physical act. Finally, after his long and bitter early life, Everett had someone with him whom he trusted with his whole heart as well as his body. It meant so much more than just carnal satisfaction when Patrick spilled inside of him with a pleasured grunt, then curled over him, the tension gone from his powerful form, as he caught his breath.

"You're so lovely and pliant first thing in the morning," Patrick said breathily, kissing Everett's shoulder and gently cupping his arse. "Though it's hardly first thing anymore. You slept late."

"It was worth it for this," Everett sighed, grinding his backside against Patrick's hand and hip. "Any chance we could—"

He was cut off by a loud knock on the flat's front door.

"What the bloody—" Patrick growled, pushing away from Everett and straightening. The knocking didn't go away when Patrick glanced over his shoulder and glared through the bedroom door and into the flat's main room. "Who the devil—" He tucked himself back into his trousers, fastening them quickly, throwing the apron back over his head for good measure, and rushing to wash his hands in the washbasin under the window as the visitor continued to knock.

Judging by the persistence of the knocking, it could only be Lionel. Everett let out a breath and collapsed to his stomach on the bed. His arse was deliciously sore and a fine layer of sweat still covered him, not to mention the fabulous slip of moisture around his hole that he would rather have liked to lie there, blissfully contemplating for a few minutes more. Whatever Lionel wanted, it had better be good.

"I'll get rid of whoever it is," Patrick said, heading into the main room and shutting the bedroom door behind him.

"That isn't going to happen," Everett said once he was alone in the room. He closed his eyes and clenched his arse for a moment, as if apologizing to it for treating it so nicely and then rushing on without giving it time to revel in its treat, then climbed off of the bed and set to work washing and dressing as fast as possible.

Sure enough, by the time he made it out to the main

room of the flat in a more or less presentable state, Lionel was seated at the kitchen table, banal smile in place, sipping a mug of tea with a bacon sandwich on a plate in front of him.

"Ah. Everett," Lionel said as though he'd been waiting at a fine hotel while Everett finished up a business meeting. "You're looking well this morning."

"It's because I've just been skillfully fucked," Everett said as though saying he'd just had his hair trimmed.

"I thought as much," Lionel replied with equal facileness. Without skipping a beat, as Patrick pointed for Everett to have a seat at the table and fixed a plate of eggs and bacon for him, Lionel went on with, "You missed an interesting morning in Darlington Gardens."

"Did we?" Everett winced slightly as he sat—which made Patrick's eyes sparkle with pride as he set a plate of breakfast at Everett's place—and reached for the coffee pot in the center of the table.

Lionel hummed as if ignoring what was right in front of him where Everett and Patrick's love life was concerned. "First off, Niall has hatched the idea of performing a Christmas panto for Stephen and Max's girls. Although, if you ask me, he's still trying to impress Blake by showering his daughters with affection."

"And why shouldn't he?" Patrick asked, taking a seat at the table with them. "It would take an act of God to separate Niall and Blake at this point, or so I understand, so why wouldn't Niall treat those girls as though they're his own?"

Lionel simply hummed, which was a sign he agreed with Patrick but didn't want to sound too conciliatory. "Regardless of the motives, your name came up as someone who would most likely give his eye teeth to star in the production."

Everett arched one brow as he sipped his coffee, deciding it needed more sugar. "Jealous that they didn't ask you?" He winked at Lionel as he plucked another sugar cube from the dish in the center of the table and added it to his mug.

Lionel screwed up his face in disgust. "How can you drink that with so much—oh, never mind. I am no actor," he said. "But I said I'd come here to ask you, even though you are already a glowing star with a captive audience." His tone was punishingly facetious. "I assume you're willing to throw your understudy a bone so that the children of Darlington Gardens can have their Christmas treat?"

Everett glanced to Patrick. He loved the idea of a pantomime for Stephen and Max's girls, perhaps even more than he loved the feverish applause he received every night at the Concord Theater. He wasn't inclined to make any decisions without Patrick's advice anymore, though.

"I think it sounds like a smashing idea," Patrick said, moving the bowl of sugar cubes out of Everett's reach when Everett moved to take another. "Anything that can be done to make children feel loved is a worthy use of time."

JUST A LITTLE CHRISTMAS

Everett smiled at him, his heart glowing with affection. One thing he and Patrick shared were miserable childhoods that had been bereft of love. Instead of reaching for another sugar cube, he took Patrick's hand and squeezed it.

"I suppose I'll tell Niall you're in, then," Lionel said, ostensibly aloof, but with a spark of approval in his blue eyes for the exchange between Everett and Patrick. Just as quickly, though, his soft manner evaporated. "Then there's the other problem," he went on. "A policeman came through the square this morning with what we all agree were nefarious intentions."

Everett's cozy mood dried up in an instant, and he frowned. "A policeman?" Anyone who meddled with his friends was an enemy, as far as he was concerned. And the residents of Darlington Gardens were some of the closest friends he had.

"Did he give his name?" Patrick asked, glowering darkly.

"Officer Richard Murdoch," Lionel reported. "He was that sour, smug sort of policeman more interested in appearing to be a big man than genuinely helping people that I cannot abide."

Patrick grunted and rubbed a hand over his face before Lionel finished speaking. "I know him," he sighed as soon as Lionel shut up. "And yes, he is a smug sort. Fancied himself better than everyone else for no goddamn reason. The man's an idiot. But what he lacks in brains he makes up for in arrogance."

Everett's brow shot up. "Why, Patrick, darling. I don't think I've heard you say so many words at once in weeks."

"I don't need words with you, love," Patrick snapped back with a look that had Everett's blood pumping hard all over again.

"Ugh, spare me." Lionel held up his hands, looking as though he'd bitten into a rotten apple. "I already have the image of an elephant mounting a gazelle in my mind whenever the two of you get started." He screwed up his face at the image, though Everett knew full well he was only having a go at them. That's what friends did, after all—had goes at each other. And after too many years of holding a stupid grudge between them, he and Lionel were back to being friends, much to everyone's benefit.

"Why, Lionel, I had no idea you thought of me as a gazelle," Everett said as though Lionel had said the sun shone out his arse.

Lionel sent him a sardonic look then picked up his mug and took a drink. Likely to hide the fond smile Everett could tell he was having a hard time suppressing. The two of them were friends once more after a silly misunderstanding had pushed them apart, and Everett loved it.

Patrick cleared his throat and rolled his eyes. "The two of you are worse than Stephen and Max's girls," he growled. He leaned back in his chair and crossed his beefy arms. "Murdoch is going to cause problems," he said.

"We all figured as much," Lionel sighed, putting

JUST A LITTLE CHRISTMAS

down his mug again. "Do you think anything can be done?"

Patrick shrugged. "Only if Murdoch is made to see that the downside to poking around where he isn't wanted is far greater than whatever benefit he thinks he might gain by exposing everyone, which is probably his aim."

"I thought people in the know were aware of what Darlington Gardens is and that they either didn't care or approved of the place," Everett said, picking up a piece of bacon and munching on it.

"The people who need to know in order for the square to evade notice know," Lionel said, "and those who would only cause trouble if they were aware don't know. That's about the best any of us can hope for." He paused, winced, then said, "Some of the others think we should inform Lord Clerkenwell of the incident."

"You don't have to go that high up yet," Patrick said. "Let Everett play his part in this panto Niall is planning. That'll give both of us a reason to loiter around the square for the next couple of weeks. If I run into Murdoch, I'll have a word with him."

Everett's insides tingled at the hint of violence in the way Patrick spoke. He was certain it was a sign of how damaged he was that whenever his lover made threats, it filled him with the urge to drop to his knees and suck the man dry.

"When does Niall plan to get started with his play,

then?" he asked Lionel to keep himself from getting all worked up when they had company.

Lionel shrugged. "Knowing Niall, as soon as possible. In fact, I was just going to head back to the square to speak with him about it, if the two of you would like to come."

Patrick narrowed his eyes. "Hold on. Isn't today the day you and David are moving into your new house in Darlington Gardens?"

"It is," Lionel said with a look that was too innocent. "Come to think of it, David could probably use a little muscle to help unload the wagons that'll be delivering our furniture and belongings all day."

Everett laughed out loud at Lionel's cunning. "I take it that's why you aren't there, then?"

"Whatever makes you say that?" Lionel reached for his mug once more.

Everett shook his head, then glanced at Patrick, loving everything about the man—from the resigned look he wore, knowing Lionel had come to recruit his muscle as well as Everett's theatrical prowess—to the kindness in his eyes that said he would spend the entire afternoon lugging furniture into a friend's house out of the goodness of his heart. Everett truly was the luckiest man alive to have found his other half.

"We are at your service," he said, finishing his last bite of bacon and standing. "Anything to help a friend."

CHAPTER 4

There were two things that Lady Margaret Evangeline Olivia Williamson was excessively proud of. The first was that she was almost ten years old. Ten was double digits. Double digits meant one was very grown up indeed. The second was that her initials spelled "MEOW", which was the sound a cat made, and cats were her favorite animals. In fact, she had asked Father Christmas to bring her a cat for Christmas—a white cat. She would tie a red ribbon with a silver bell around its neck and call it Snowy. And since Papa insisted Father Christmas would find them at their new home in Darlington Gardens—and Niall assured her that Father Christmas read every letter good little girls sent him—Greta knew the cat was all but hers.

"I told Father Christmas to bring you a black cat to match my Snowy," Greta informed Jessie as the two of them rifled through the downstairs linen closet in search of old blankets with which to build beds for their antici-pated new arrivals. "You can name it Sooty."

"But I want a puppy, not a kitten," Jessie said with a frown. "Jane says that Mutty needs a playmate so that he stops chewing everyone's shoes."

Greta rolled her eyes and fixed her sister with a flat stare, the way their mama always had whenever Papa said something she thought was silly. Which was practi-cally everything Papa ever said. Which was why Greta was happy her mother and that horrible Mr. Archibald were gone. Though they should have given Alan to Papa to look after along with her and Jessie.

"If Mutty needs a playmate, Sir and Max should get one for the orphanage," Greta said before sticking her head back into the closet. "Snowy will need Sooty as a playmate here."

After a pause, Jessie asked, "Why are they called 'Sir' and 'Max'? Why don't we call them Mr. Siddel and... whatever Max's surname is, like we call Mr. Long 'Mr. Long' and Mr. Piper 'Mr. Piper'?"

Greta pulled her head out of the closet with another, irritated sigh. On the one hand, the problem with living in a brand new house filled with brand new things was that there weren't any old blankets to make a bed for a cat out of. On the other, Jessie was being annoying, as little sisters were want to be.

"'Sir' is because he's headmaster of the orphanage," she explained in her best grown-up voice. "And 'Max' is because that's what he told everyone to call him. Jane

JUST A LITTLE CHRISTMAS

said so, and Jane is in love with him, so she would know."

"I thought Max was in love with Sir," Jessie said, tilting her head to the side and scrunching up her face.

"Well, he is." Greta deflated from her imperiousness a little. "But I think he loves Jane too, only differently."

"We could always ask him who he loves more," Jessie said thoughtfully. "He and Sir, and Mr. Jewel and Mr. Wrexham and Mr. Lionel are downstairs in the parlor having tea with Papa and Niall."

Greta caught her breath. "Did Mr. Lionel bring sweeties?" Mr. Lionel always brought sweeties with him when he visited the orphanage.

She grabbed Jessie's hand, abandoning the linen closet, and tearing down the stairs. When they lived in Yorkshire, it was always a special occasion when grown-ups visited Papa. They visited Mama all the time, but Mama never let them speak with the guests. Papa, on the other hand, never failed to introduce them to new people and to ask them questions. Now that they lived in Darlington Gardens, Papa and Niall had guests all the time, and they were the most delightful people Greta had ever known. Most of them were theater people, who were the very best people, as far as Greta was concerned.

As they reached the bottom of the stairs and approached the parlor, Greta slowed down. The grown-ups sounded far too serious for them to burst in with questions about love.

"At least he hasn't been back since yesterday," Mr.

Wrexham said in his big, deep voice. Mr. Wrexham was the biggest man she knew, even bigger than the strongman at the faire Papa had taken them to two summers ago. "Perhaps he doesn't think it's worth his time to meddle."

"Men like that always think meddling is worth their time," Mr. Lionel said.

"I agree," Niall seconded. "That sort makes our lives much more difficult than they need to be. They're intent on ruining us."

"I'd like to see them try." Mr. Jewel sounded as powerful and awe-inspiring in their parlor as he did on the stage. Greta rushed to the doorway so she could get a look at him. Sure enough, he looked magnificent in a festive, green suit, and he wore kohl around his eyes, making them look blue and magical. In fact, she was convinced Mr. Jewel was a sorcerer of some sort.

"I will never understand why so many people find it so necessary to attempt to interfere with our lives when they barely know who we are to begin with," Papa said, shaking his head.

"Which is why we have to be unerringly careful about our Christmas celebrations." Niall nodded to Papa and took his hand. The way he smiled at Papa made Greta smile too. Finally, someone cared for Papa as much as she, Jessie, and Alan did.

"Well, you can have the party and your show at our house," Mr. Long said in his happy, booming voice from the far corner of the room. He was the only one of the

46

JUST A LITTLE CHRISTMAS

guests who stood and paced around while everyone else sat. Greta couldn't remember seeing Mr. Long sit down or stay still once. He was as bad as Mutty that way. "No one will bat an eye at Phoebe and I hosting the orphans for a party. And if half the men in attendance are wearing dresses and kissing under the mistletoe, I'll just blame it on particularly good beer."

"A party?" Jessie gasped at Greta's side.

In an instant, all of the grown-ups turned to them. Greta couldn't understand why, for the life of her, they all looked so upset. Except, perhaps they'd intended the party to be a surprise.

"I'm sorry, Papa," she said, grabbing Jessie's hand and stepping into the room. "We just came to ask Max a question. We didn't expect to hear anything we weren't supposed to."

"It's all right, darlings." Papa stood, hurrying to give them a hug, though he looked a bit nervous as he did. Then again, Papa often looked nervous. He still missed Alan and was working hard to get him back.

"You have a question for me?" Max stood from where he and Sir had been sitting next to each other on the sofa. He let go of Sir's hand and came to meet them near the doorway.

"Yes." Jessie's brow furrowed into a serious look. "Who do you love more, Sir or Jane?"

Greta blinked and glanced curiously up at Max. She did not expect for Max's face to go red, for him to stammer, or for him to take a few steps back and look at Sir, as if he didn't know the answer to a math problem. She didn't expect the other grown-ups to suddenly go over all squirrely either.

"I think it's time for us to go," Mr. Wrexham said, nodding to Mr. Jewel, who followed him hurriedly out to the hall.

"And David needs my help arranging all the furniture we brought in yesterday," Mr. Lionel said, scurrying past them. "Goodbye, my cheeky, little loves," he said to Greta and Jessie as he left, pulling two small lollies from his pocket and handing them to the girls as he left.

Mr. Long was laughing as though someone had made a joke, but he, too, headed out of the room, slapping Papa on the shoulder as he went. "Best of luck answering all their questions," he said with a snorting laugh.

Greta had never seen a room full of grown-ups clear out so fast. It wasn't until Papa cleared his throat and said, "Girls, why don't you sit down so we can have a talk," that she realized Max hadn't answered Jessie's question before leaving too.

"Ooh! Chocolate biscuits!" Jessie rushed to the table where the grown-ups' tea set was laid out. "Can I have one?" she asked, even though she already had the lolly Mr. Lionel had given her in her mouth.

"Yes, darling, but do sit down," Papa said. "We need to have a word about something very important." He sent a look to Niall that Greta couldn't decide if it was worried or teasing.

Niall seemed to be having a hard time not laughing,

JUST A LITTLE CHRISTMAS

even though his face had gone bright pink, the way it did whenever Greta caught the two of them kissing. She liked the way Niall kissed Papa too. Mama never once kissed him that she knew about, and Papa so clearly liked to be kissed.

Greta had a seat on the couch where Sir and Max had been sitting. Jessie settled next to her, handing her a chocolate biscuit. Greta thanked her and slipped the lolly into the pocket of her pinafore so she could nibble on the biscuit. Papa and Niall sat side by side on the couch across from them. The party was definitely supposed to be a surprise, Greta decided. Papa and Niall looked anxious that the surprise had been ruined.

"We've been meaning to have a word with the two of you about something very important for a while," Papa said, looking very serious indeed.

"Yes," Niall agreed, nodding to Papa before addressing her and Jessie. "We didn't think it needed to be said, but after the policeman showed up in Darlington Gardens, and after…the other thing that happened yesterday morning…." His voice went gruff and his face turned even redder as he glanced to Jessie, and he cleared his throat.

Greta frowned and thought about yesterday morning. They'd gone to the orphanage, like they always did. That wasn't unusual. Other than that, the only thing she could remember was Papa telling Jessie that Father Christmas would know where to find them.

She sucked in a breath. Was Father Christmas

MERRY FARMER

himself coming to the party Mr. Long was planning to host?

"You see, darlings," Papa went on, his face as red as the holly berries decorating the mantel of the parlor's fireplace, "there are things we should say to others and things we shouldn't."

"Some things that we should only share within Darlington Gardens that are unwise to talk about with strangers who live outside the square," Niall added.

Greta nodded, matching the gravity of her papa and Niall, but inside she squealed. They were definitely talking about the party. It must be exclusive, like the sort of party Mama always loved to go to, and only people from Darlington Gardens were to be invited.

"Like, for example," Papa said, glancing to Niall with a stilted gesture, "it would be unwise to tell people that your papa shares a bedroom with Niall."

"Or that we sometimes kiss each other," Niall added, shifting his shoulders strangely.

Greta frowned. She wasn't sure what *that* had to do with the Christmas party. Hadn't Mr. Long said he would hang mistletoe at the party so that people could kiss? People kissed all the time, or so Greta had discovered since Papa and Niall had moved them to London. Maybe they didn't kiss in Yorkshire, but she'd seen plenty of kissing at the Concord Theater on the days Papa and Niall took them there while Niall worked. She'd seen Miss Florence kissing Mr. Juniper, Mr. Martin kissing Mr. Forrester, and Miss Lily kissing Miss Vera. And at

JUST A LITTLE CHRISTMAS

home, in Darlington Gardens, everyone was very kissy. Max made her and Jessie and Jane and Katie giggle all the time, he was so silly about stealing kisses from Sir when they thought no one was looking. And Mr. Long had kissed Lady Phoebe in the park just the other day while the orphanage was at recess.

Perhaps Papa thought it was unusual that he and Niall slept in the same bed. Or that they were in love with each other. It was true that she hadn't realized men could be in love with other men when they lived in Yorkshire—and Mama and horrible Mr. Archibald seemed to think it was a wicked thing—but didn't the Bible say that David and Jonathan loved each other so much that they had one soul? And wasn't John the disciple whom Jesus loved? Most of the men who lived in Darlington Gardens were in love with the men they lived with. And Jane and Katie said Max and Sir shared a bed too, even though there were plenty of rooms in the orphanage.

No, they must have been talking about the Christmas party. The party was obviously meant to be a secret.

"So you understand why discretion is so important?" Papa asked, making Greta realize she hadn't been paying attention as much as she should have. He glanced to Niall—who was now holding his hand—then back to her.

"Yes, Papa, of course," Greta said with a somber nod. "It's a secret. Only people in Darlington Gardens should know."

"Exactly." Papa let out a breath, looking relieved. He stood, leaning across the space, and kissed Greta's forehead, then Jessie's. "You understand why no one outside of the square needs to know too, don't you, love?"

"Yes, I supposed," Jessie answered with a confused frown.

"Good." Papa kissed them each again, then stood straight, turning to Niall. "And now, we have quite a few preparations to make. Christmas is less than a fortnight away."

That decided things for Greta. She stood with a broad smile. The entire conversation had definitely been about the party.

"I know it's Saturday and there are no lessons today, but can Jessie and I go play at the orphanage?" she asked, her heart racing at the idea of telling Jane and Katie everything she'd learned.

"I don't see why not," Papa said, glancing to Niall with a funny sparkle in his eyes. "That is to say, the house would be empty, since Xavier is visiting a friend in Marylebone and Mr. Bolton won't be back to get supper started for a few hours at least. And the new maid doesn't start until Monday."

"Yes, I think it would be a lovely idea for the two of you to spend the entire afternoon at the orphanage," Niall said in a rushed voice, smiling fondly at Papa.

Greta's excitement grew. She grabbed Jessie's hand and tugged her out to the hall to fetch their coats, hats, and gloves.

"Do you need us to walk you over to the orphanage?" Papa asked, coming out of the parlor with Niall.

JUST A LITTLE CHRISTMAS

"No, it's only two doors down," Greta told him.

"I think most of the girls are in the park this afternoon anyhow," Niall said. "We're on supervision duty tomorrow afternoon, by the way."

Greta barely heard him, she was in such a hurry to put her winter things on. "Come on," she whispered to Jessie as they bundled up. "We have to tell Jane and Katie about the party."

"What party?" Jessie asked, her confused frown still in place.

Greta peeked at Papa and Niall hurrying up the stairs, holding hands, and giggled. "The secret Christmas party Papa and Niall were talking about in there," she said,

"Is that what Papa meant by keeping secrets?"

"Yes," Greta giggled.

Jessie was buttoning her coat wrong, so Greta batted her hands away to rebutton it for her. "But Papa said not to tell anyone."

"Anyone outside of Darlington Gardens," Greta corrected her. "Jane and Katie are part of the square, so we can tell them everything."

"Oh, right."

The two of them burst into giggles and dashed out through the front door. It was a sunny afternoon, and even though it was cold, the girls from the orphanage were mostly playing in the park that made up the center of their square. Greta loved the park. It was much smaller than the grounds of Selby House, but unlike

MERRY FARMER

Yorkshire, they were allowed to sit and climb on the benches, run down the paths, spin hoops, throw balls, and play hopscotch instead of just looking at things without touching. Mutty was running around with several of the other girls, and just as Greta had hoped, Jane and Katie were outside, drawing on the pavement with chalk they had probably swiped from the orphanage's classrooms.

"Guess what?" Greta gasped as soon as she and Jessie made their way into the gated park and up to Jane and Katie.

"Chicken butt?" Jane answered back.

The four of them laughed loudly together. Nice Mr. Silver—who wore kohl, powder, and lip rouge like a woman—shook his head at them as he walked among the girls. He, Mr. Tarlington, and Annie Ross appeared to be the grown-ups who were in charge of minding the children and keeping them safe that day. Mr. Lionel was there as well, pushing swings for some of the other girls... which was odd to Greta, since he'd said he needed to go back to his house to help Mr. Wirth arrange furniture. But grown-ups were peculiar sometimes.

Greta moved to sit on the cold stone pavement with Jane and Katie. Jessie sat as well, and the four of them formed a closed circle. "Papa and Niall and Sir and Max and Mr. Long and a lot of the other grown-ups are planning a surprise Christmas party for us."

Jane and Katie gasped, their eyes going wide at the idea.

54

"And Father Christmas is invited," Greta added, then squealed with excitement.

Katie squealed as well, but Jane rocked back on her haunches, crossing her arms. "There's no such thing as Father Christmas, silly."

Greta's mouth dropped open. "Take that back!"

"There is too a Father Christmas," Jessie said at the same time.

"Is not," Jane grumbled.

Greta *humphed* and lifted to her knees. "Mr. Silver, is there such a thing as Father Christmas?" she called to him.

Mr. Silver smiled brightly and said, "Of course, there's a Father Christmas, sweetheart."

"Thank you, Mr. Silver," Greta called back, then turned to Jane with a self-satisfied look. "See?"

Jane didn't look convinced, but Greta didn't care.

"I have an idea about the party," she said, gathering the four of them back into their circle.

The issue of Father Christmas was forgotten as they put their heads together.

"Papa and Niall and Sir and Max and Mr. Long and everyone else have been very kind to us this year," she went on.

"They sure have," Katie said, eyes round, nodding. "They built us this new home when the other one burned down."

"They saved all the girls and boys from the factories," Jane added, looking haunted.

MERRY FARMER

Greta knew something had happened to Jane over the summer, but they'd been having so much fun playing in the weeks since she and Jessie and Papa and Niall had moved to Darlington Gardens that she hadn't thought to ask.

"And Mama ran away with horrible Mr. Archibald who hit me, and they took Alan, and they still have Alan with them," Jessie added in a sad voice.

"So I think we should do something nice for them," Greta went on.

The other three lit up and smiled.

"Like what?" Katie asked.

Greta let out a breath and scratched her head. "I don't know. But we should do something for them. At the party."

"We could make them presents?" Jane asked.

"We don't have any money," Katie told her, then said, "We could draw them pictures."

"That would be nice," Greta said.

"We could do a play for them because they are doing a play for us," Jessie said, then added, "Niall and Papa have been writing songs for it after we go to bed. Or, at least, they were last night. Until they stopped playing the piano so they could kiss."

Something about that made Greta feel funny and giddy and a little wiggly and uncomfortable, so she ignored it and said, "Maybe Mr. Lionel will know what we should do."

JUST A LITTLE CHRISTMAS

All four of them sat taller, turning to the swings where Mr. Lionel was laughing along with Lori and Ivy.

"Mr. Lionel likes fun and games," Katie agreed. "We should definitely ask him."

They all stood and scurried over to the swings, slipping on a few patches of ice as they did.

"Mr. Lionel, Mr. Lionel, we need your help," Greta asked when they reached the swings. She didn't even mind that Lori and Ivy were there, paying attention to what they were saying.

"How can I help you beautiful, wicked creatures?" Mr. Lionel asked.

Greta giggled. Mr. Lionel was delightfully silly. He sounded like a girl, and sometimes he acted like one too, but he made her feel comfortable and protected more than most of the men in Darlington Gardens.

"We know Papa and Niall's secret," Greta announced, clapping her hands.

"O-oh?" Mr. Lionel looked suddenly uneasy.

"Yes," Jessie said. "They're planning a Christmas party for us."

"A secret Christmas party," Jane added.

"And Father Christmas is invited," Katie finished, as though that were the shining glory of the whole thing.

"Ohh." Mr. Lionel drew out the sound, breaking into a wide—and a little bit relieved—smile. He leaned in closer—and Lori and Ivy jumped off their swings to lean in closer too—and said, "You're right. They are."

"We want to surprise all the grown-ups with something grand," Greta said.

"But we don't know what," Jane added.

"Since they've been so kind to us this year," Katie finished again.

"I think that's a beautiful idea," Mr. Lionel said. "And I might have an idea of just the thing you could do that they would adore."

"Oh, really?" Greta pressed her hands to her heart, so glad they'd thought to ask Mr. Lionel for help. "We'd be ever so grateful if you could help us with something."

"I would love to help you, darling." Mr. Lionel beamed at each of them in turn. "We'll surprise everyone in a way they won't ever forget."

CHAPTER 5

"You will never guess what the little rapscallions of this square are up to," Lionel said as he marched through the front door and into his and David's lovely new home. The house was a scene of chaos at the moment, with furniture thrown into rooms every which way, stacks of crates that needed unpacking, and bits of straw and sawdust from the remover's wagons and from packing strewn over everything. He slowed his steps and glanced warily at the floor as he proceeded through the foyer and into the parlor, where David was unpacking books.

"You are correct," David said, taking the stack in his arms to the shelf he'd set up on one side of the room. "With you involved, I'd never guess."

Lionel paused to appreciate the long, lean lines of his husband's body as he reached to put books on the top shelf. David was as fine a specimen of masculinity as had ever been created. His broad shoulders and back were strong, his arms were muscular enough to suit Lionel's tastes without being burly, and his backside was as firm and tight as Lionel could have asked for. All the parts of David that weren't currently on display were perfect enough to make his mouth water as well. He considered himself truly blessed to have thrown his lot in with a man as utterly bewitching and flawless as David. To the rest of the world, they were only business partners, but Lionel would be damned if he considered David anything less than his husband.

"Would you care to stop ogling my backside and help unpack these boxes?" David asked without even turning to check whether Lionel was ogling. "You've been avoiding helping me set up the house for days now."

A fond grin spread across Lionel's lips as he unbuttoned his winter coat. "I haven't been avoiding anything," Lionel lied. "I've been serving as ambassador in our new community." He shrugged out of his coat and took it back to the foyer to hang it and his hat on the stand by the door alongside David's winter things.

When he stepped back into the parlor, David was heading over to the crates of books. He marched right past them and up to Lionel instead of continuing to unpack. As he met Lionel near the doorway, he slipped an arm around Lionel's waist and tugged him close for a surprise kiss.

Lionel gasped at first, then sighed with delight and melted against David, letting the man have his way with

JUST A LITTLE CHRISTMAS

his mouth and tongue. David was the only man who had ever had the power to turn his knees to jelly with a single kiss, and Lionel had been with so many men before David that he'd lost track. Or rather, he couldn't remember a single one of his former lovers now that he belonged to David.

"If that's the thanks I get for avoiding helping you unpack and arrange the house," he began with a breathy sigh, sliding his arms over David's shoulders, "then let me just fetch my coat and return to the park so that I can come back later for more."

"Absolutely not, you little French whore," David growled, equal parts affection and teasing in his deep voice. He pulled away enough to pivot behind Lionel and nudge him toward the crates, smacking his backside hard as he did. "Get to work."

Lionel yelped playfully at the spank, shivering and overheated in seconds. "I thought you liked those tricks I picked up in France," he said with a coquettish look over his shoulder.

David laughed and shook his head. "They aren't particularly handy when it comes to shelving books and arranging furniture. Unless your prick is so hard you can lift a sofa with it."

"It's getting there," Lionel flirted, lowering his voice to a purr.

David laughed louder and returned to the crate for another armful of books. He sent Lionel a look that promised they would end the conversation in a horizontal

MERRY FARMER

position…if Lionel did as he was told and helped. "So what would I not believe that the Darlington girls are up to?" he asked as the two of them went about their work.

Lionel's heart felt as light as falling snow as he took three books from one of the crates and followed David to the shelves. Of course, he was teasing David by pretending to be a lazy bugger. If it would have made his love happy, he would have constructed the house himself, brick by brick, without taking a break for rest or food until the task was done. Well, perhaps tea. One had to have tea. The point was that David was far more amused by Lionel's silly antics than he was impressed by the myriad of far more powerful things Lionel was capable of. David was far too serious for anyone's good health to begin with, and Lionel considered it his mission in life to keep a smile on his husband's face. In their bedroom and out of it.

"Those clever darlings of Blake's have figured out that we're planning a surprise Christmas party for them," Lionel explained. "The minxes heard everything when they were listening in on the meeting we had earlier."

"Yes, I heard that the younger one in particular has a penchant for being places she shouldn't be at inconvenient times," David said, clearing his throat, second-hand embarrassment coloring his cheeks in a way Lionel found so charming he actually took five books from the crate on his second trip.

"Anyone foolish enough to have children in the house without putting locks on his bedroom door deserves all of

JUST A LITTLE CHRISTMAS

the embarrassment he gets," Lionel said sagely, reaching across David to put his books on the shelf—or rather, putting his books on a part of the shelf that would allow him to scoot as close to David as possible while doing it.

David sent him a flat, sideways look that could have been in answer to his statement or his gesture. He headed back to the now empty crate and moved it and a few others to the side of the room, then pointed for Lionel to take the other end of one of the matching set of sofas they'd purchased for the room so they could move it into place.

"Niall said he had a locksmith install a lock yesterday," he said as he lifted his end of the sofa.

Lionel proved he was more than just a pretty face by lifting his end of the sofa with ease and helping David position it where he wanted it. "A wise man. Regardless, those charming imps and their friends from the orphanage came to me, asking if I would help them plot a counter-surprise for Niall and Blake and Stephen and Max, and likely everyone else under the sun as well, because they have been so kind to them all this year."

David looked surprised as he straightened and studied the placement of the sofa, then glanced at Lionel. His eyes softened when they met Lionel's. "That's quite sweet of those girls."

"I thought so as well," Lionel smiled. "Which is why I offered to teach them a special Christmas song to sing at the party."

MERRY FARMER

David arched an eyebrow. "Your song had better be appropriate for children."

Lionel stepped around the end of the sofa, swaying closer to David. "Now why would you simply assume any song I would teach to children would be inappropriate in any way?" When he came close enough, he walked his fingers up David's chest, unbuttoning the top button of his waistcoat as he did, and fixed David with a sultry look. He leaned closer, bringing his lips close to David's.

"Who's the minx now?" David growled, sliding a hand across Lionel's hip.

"I picked up a fresh supply of French letters from the chemist yesterday," Lionel said in return, arching one eyebrow invitingly.

"Did you?" David's hand continued around to Lionel's backside.

Lionel was thoroughly ready to be ravished in every way and tilted his head toward David's to indicate as much when a flash of movement outside one of the windows caught his eye. By instinct, he pulled back with a frown, turning to see what had intrinsically alarmed him so much.

A man had just stepped up to the uncurtained window. He held his hands to the glass to shade whatever glare the noonday sun had created as he peered into the room. Lionel and David leapt away from each other, and Lionel's blood boiled as he recognized the face of the

64

policeman who had caused so much trouble a few days before.

"Curtains," David grumbled, then cleared his throat. "We're putting the curtains up next."

"Only a fool carries on like a ninny in a ground-floor room before putting the curtains up," Lionel agreed, as though he wasn't the one who had initiated the intimacy. "And only a coward fails to give a snooping bastard a piece of his mind when he intrudes on a private moment."

He started for the hallway with determined strides, grabbing his coat and hat from the rack in the foyer.

"Lionel, don't bring trouble down on yourself." David followed him, grabbing his coat and hat as well.

"Darling, trouble brings itself down on me," Lionel replied with a challenging arch of one eyebrow before darting out into the frosty square.

Officer Murdoch was back. Lionel had figured it was only a matter of time. The bastard had the nerve to strut into the square with billy club in hand. Whether he'd seen more than he should have between Lionel and David or not, he now seemed fixated on the children playing in the park. Or perhaps he was interested in the men taking their turn supervising the play.

"You," Lionel called to him, intercepting Murdoch at the corner of the park, across the street from his and David's house. "What are you doing here?"

"Lionel," David cautioned him, catching up to Lionel's side.

Several other Darlington Gardens residents had stopped what they were doing to note Murdoch's presence. Xavier Lawrence peeled away from his conversation with Barry Townsend to race a few doors down to the orphanage, and then on to Niall and Blake's house, once Stephen Siddel stepped outside to see what was happening. Word of anything out of the ordinary spread like lightning in the square.

"For your information," Murdoch said with an imperious air, tapping his club against his palm, "this area has been flagged as a place of suspicion."

Lionel narrowed his eyes, seething with hatred for Murdoch and everything he stood for. "Is that so?" he asked, crossing his arms. "It looks like a play area for children to me."

He glanced into the park, where several groups of girls from the orphanage, Blake's daughters, and a few friends who Lionel believed were children of the servants who worked in some of the nearby houses, were playing. The sounds of laughter and shrieking, songs, skipping ropes, and even a recorder flute that some wicked soul had entrusted to one of the girls rang through the air. The children didn't seem to have a care in the world, though the adults who watched them inside the park were all instantly on the alert.

"Don't it seem strange to you to have all them kiddies here and plenty of men, but no mummies or nurses?" Murdoch drawled in his East London accent.

"Not at all," Lionel glared at him, "when one

considers that that building there is an orphanage." He nodded to Stephen's place. Max had joined Stephen on the front stoop. The two had their heads together and were whispering as they watched Murdoch.

"Huh." Murdoch didn't seem at all deterred. "Don't it seem strange to you that there are no women living hereabouts?"

"I beg your pardon?" The offended question came from James Tarleton, who was dressed in full drag as he supervised the girls, and who made the most convincing woman Lionel had ever known.

Murdoch blinked at the interruption, his eyes going wide at the sight of James. He broke into a saucy smile. "Begging your pardon, miss." He tipped his hat to her, then went on with, "You're quite a looker," then winked.

James giggled and preened, flirting right back. Lionel would have found the entire exchange diverting, if he weren't so furious at Murdoch's ignominious intent.

"This is a private neighborhood, officer." David beat him to his reply. "And as you can see, the children who live here, both at the orphanage and in families in residence, have ample protection as part of a coordinated supervision effort."

"Why hire one nursemaid when you can rely on everyone on the square to care for each other as a community," Lionel added through clenched teeth.

Murdoch quit flirting with James and made a sour face at Lionel. "Hold on. This isn't one of them newfan-

MERRY FARMER

gled socialist communes what keeps popping up all over, is it?"

Lionel glanced to David to see whether he thought it would be more or less dangerous to leave Murdoch with the impression they were a political community. Heaven only knew there were communes and societies and mutual support organizations of every kind imaginable sprouting up all over England and the continent these days as old ways gave way to new.

"It's a neighborhood," David answered, crossing his arms.

Lionel loved him to distraction. David was quick as well as clever. As crafty as Lionel knew he was—and he was certain he could have worked out a way to get rid of Murdoch on his own—having David there to combine forces with made them an unstoppable team.

Murdoch sniffed and rubbed his stubbly chin, as though making up his mind about whether he would take David at his word or not. "If it's all the same to you, boys, I'll just have a look around. To keep the kiddies safe and all." He nodded into the park, but his gaze lingered on James.

"I'm certain Miss Flora would be happy to show you around and keep an eye on you," Lionel said, using James's stage name.

"I most certainly would," James said in his sweetest, most feminine voice, returning Lionel's unspoken request with a look of steel. Murdoch wouldn't step an inch out of line with James keeping him in check.

JUST A LITTLE CHRISTMAS

"David, I believe we have business with Mr. Long," Lionel went on, meeting David's eyes with a determined look. Danny technically owned the square, after all, and even though Lionel was loath to bring in outside help, a man like Danny might actually have the clout to get rid of Murdoch.

"Yes, we do," David answered. He nodded to Murdoch. "Good day, sir."

Murdoch was too busy making eyes at James to bother to reply, so David and Lionel walked around him and headed to the opposite end of the square, where Danny's enormous townhouse stood.

Danny and Lady Phoebe's butler was a member of The Brotherhood—as were a large majority of the servants at work in the houses of Darlington Gardens— and let them in on sight. Lionel and David weren't the only guests the Longs had that day either. Everett and Patrick hadn't gone home after the meeting at Niall and Blake's house. They were there with Danny and Lady Phoebe, and, for some reason, Martin Piper as well, in the ballroom that stretched along the entire side of the first floor of the massive house. By the look of things, the way Everett stood with arms outstretched at one end of the room and the way Martin was arranging chairs, they were scouting the space where their pantomime would be performed. Lionel was rather interested in the space as well, since the girls would perform their song for the adults once the panto was done.

69

"Halt! Who goes there?" Everett boomed from his makeshift stage.

"Someone who doesn't have time for your nonsense, Jewel," Lionel called back to him, pretending to be even more put out than he was. Paradoxically, sparring with Everett actually improved his mood after the encounter with Murdoch.

"We've just had another run-in with Officer Murdoch," David told them, getting down to business.

"Bloody fucking hell," Danny cursed.

"Darling," Lady Phoebe scolded him, resting one hand on his arm and the other on her hugely pregnant belly. She shook her head.

"Sorry." Danny looked adorably sheepish at her scolding before squaring his shoulders and frowning. "That bas—gentleman is back again?"

"Did anyone really think he *wouldn't* come back?" Martin asked, somehow making the question sound cheerful, as was Martin's unique talent.

"I was hoping he'd get bored," David sighed. "But I wasn't counting on it."

"James is keeping him busy as he pokes around the park," Lionel said, then grinned. "I wouldn't be surprised if James gets a poke around the park for her troubles."

Everett snorted with laughter, but Patrick grumbled, "That's the last thing we need. Murdoch wouldn't respond well to what James's got under her silk knickers."

"No, he would not," David agreed. "Fortunately, James is smart enough not to let things go there."

"But I doubt Murdoch is smart enough to leave well enough alone," Patrick added.

"What do we do?" Lady Phoebe asked, glancing from Patrick to David to her husband. Lionel was extraordinarily fond of the woman and the genuine concern she showed for their lot. A woman of Lady Phoebe's wealth and position didn't have to give a fig about any of them. But after the maelstrom of twists and turns that made up Lady Phoebe's own life, she'd become a firm champion for the downtrodden and endangered.

"We couldn't form a perimeter of some sort to keep the likes of Murdoch out, could we?" Martin suggested, finishing with the chairs and coming to join them.

"I'm afraid any overt show of resistance we make will only encourage the man," Patrick said, scowling into space as though considering the problem.

"We can't go jumping at shadows every time someone wanders through the square," Lionel insisted. "That rather defeats the point of having a safe neighborhood."

"I hate to say it, but I think we're going to have to get Jack involved," Danny sighed, rubbing a hand over his face.

Lionel hissed in irritation. "I detest the notion of calling daddy every time we have so much as a stubbed toe." Though even he was beginning to see that they needed the most powerful weapon in their arsenal if they were going to not only stop Murdoch, but prevent others like him from getting any ideas in the future.

MERRY FARMER

"Lord Clerkenwell is rather like a father figure, or at least a headmaster," Lady Phoebe said with a grin. "But Bianca has him wrapped around her little finger."

"I'd put my trust in Lady Bianca Clerkenwell to save us all any day," Lionel laughed suddenly. "In fact, why don't we set her up at one of the square's entrances with a billy club of her own to ward off any troublemakers." The image of Lady Bianca's ferocity put to work protecting all of them was enough to lighten Lionel's mood considerably.

"I'll pay a call on Bianca this afternoon," Lady Phoebe said, starting away from the others.

"You'll do no such thing." Danny grabbed her arm gently to stop her. "You're about ready to burst, woman. You'll stay right here, where I can keep an eye on you. Lady Bianca will come here."

Lady Phoebe's cheeks went pink and she smiled fondly at her husband, but also rolled her eyes. "He was like this with our firstborn too," she told Lionel and David. "I won't have a moment's peace until he or she is safe in their cradle."

"And then you won't have a moment's peace as we get started on the next one," Danny growled, tugging her into an embrace.

Lionel sent David a fake sardonic look, though seeing such a happy couple building a family filled him with the sort of domestic joy he secretly adored. "Well, if you all are determined to drag Lord Clerkenwell into this mess instead of having the lot of us solve it ourselves, then

JUST A LITTLE CHRISTMAS

David and I should go home and start working on our own brood."

Lady Phoebe blinked at him in baffled surprise.

"What he means is that we still have a great deal of furniture to arrange and boxes to unpack," David told her with a scolding look for Lionel.

"Yes, that's exactly what I mean," Lionel said in a voice that conveyed anything but, flickering an eyebrow at David.

"You were about to shock the poor woman into going into labor early," David muttered to him as they headed across the square and back to their own house several minutes later.

"Nonsense," Lionel sniffed. "Lady Phoebe is much more of a woman of the world than people give her credit for. I merely surprised her with a comment she wasn't expecting."

David laughed and shook his head. He reached for Lionel's hand, but pulled back as Murdoch's ribald laughter sounded from somewhere inside the garden. A moment later, they spotted him pushing James on one of the swings while the girls from the orphanage watched, giggling.

"Perhaps we should sic the girls on Murdoch," Lionel said, tilting his head to the side in consideration. "There's nothing like a pack of wild girls to defend one's home territory."

David chuckled, reaching for Lionel's hand in earnest as they climbed their front steps and let themselves inside. It wasn't lost on Lionel that they hadn't felt the need to lock the door when they left earlier. Darlington Gardens truly was a safe place for them.

"I live in mortal terror of those girls," David admitted as they removed their coats. As soon as everything was hanging on the rack, David scooped an arm around Lionel's waist and pressed their bodies together. "Now," he said in a low growl, his mouth suddenly a breath away from Lionel's, "what's this about a new supply of French letters you've just purchased?"

Lionel let out a breath of surrender that turned into a sultry laugh before he closed the distance between them, slanting his mouth over David's. He truly was the most fortunate man in the world.

CHAPTER 6

Writing and staging a two-hour musical with a male and female chorus and half a dozen solo parts for the Concord Theater was as simple as a puzzle with three pieces compared to writing a fifteen-minute Christmas pantomime and teaching the songs to the peacocks of Darlington Gardens. Or so Niall was convinced as yet another rehearsal ran long, thanks to the egos involved.

"Why doesn't Robin Hood have a solo in the first act?" Everett asked in an irritated voice as the chorus of merry men finished the last note of the number they all sang to open the show. "Surely, a character like *the* Robin Hood should get to sing by himself for more than the verses of this number."

"The play is only fifteen minutes long," Niall reminded him from his seat on the piano bench beside Blake, who had signed on to accompany the production.

Niall rubbed his temples, wondering why he had cast Everett in the starring role. But, of course, if he hadn't cast Everett, he never would have heard the end of it.

"I'll take thirty seconds of glory if I can get it," Everett insisted.

"I've heard that about you," James—who was playing Maid Marion—hummed.

"Darling," Everett flirted back to her, "with me, you only need thirty seconds."

"Before you start laughing," Patrick finished in an undertone.

The room burst into laughter, which was a relief, as far as Niall was concerned. Anyone who flirted with Everett when Patrick was in the room was taking their life in their hands. Fortunately for them all, Patrick was in a merry mood. Likely because he'd actually succeeded in turning Officer Murdoch away from nosing around the square for the fourth day in a row just by standing in the middle of the road near one of the entrances and glaring at him.

Though from the whispers Niall had heard lately, Officer Murdoch was equally as intent on courting "Miss Flora" now as he was determined to catch one of the residents of Darlington Gardens doing something that would allow him to raid the whole damn place.

"Let me just remind you that Christmas is in less than a week," Niall told the full complement of his cast as they squashed into the parlor he and Blake had converted into a music room, "and Stephen can only keep the children occupied at the orphanage for so long this afternoon. We need to finish rehearsal on a strong note before the girls flood out into the park for playtime and get suspicious."

Greta and Jessie were suspicious enough already. They'd spent the last week floating around the house with grins and giggles, dropping hints about all the gifts they expected Father Christmas to bring because they had been very good indeed and not whispered a word about anything they weren't supposed to talk about. Niall went hot and cold every time he thought about the things Blake's girls knew that they weren't supposed to and the possibilities of what might happen if they talked out of turn.

"Fine!" Everett sighed dramatically. "I suppose I could be content with mere verses between this splendid chorus. Carry on, maestro!" He was close enough to the piano to slap Blake on the back.

"Ow," Blake mumbled. "Careful with all those rings, man." He rubbed his shoulder, grinning at Niall as he did, then playing the opening bars of the show's finale.

Niall grinned fondly at him as the full cast belted out the final number. He wasn't sure he'd ever seen Blake so happy in his life. It wasn't just the two of them back together or the girls safe—though he was certain Blake would have been even happier if they had Alan as well and a divorce from Annamarie. It was the entire community of Darlington Gardens. Blake had lived his entire life believing he was an anomaly, that very few men like them existed, and that he would never feel at home in his own skin. It was a joy unlike anything Niall had ever experienced to watch Blake come to life as he realized not only that he wasn't an aberration, he was a vital member of a large and supportive brotherhood.

The final, ringing crescendo of the pantomime's finale underscored the joy in Niall's soul. The men of the cast sang it with gusto, all of them seemingly just as happy as Blake and just as content to have found a place where they belonged. Darlington Gardens truly was a special little slice of London, and Niall was bound and determined to keep it that way, no matter what troubles they ran into.

"Very good," he said, applauding as he stood from the piano bench. "We'll start dress rehearsals at the Longs' tomorrow afternoon."

"Finally," James said with a dramatic sigh. "I simply cannot wait for you all to see the confections Irene and I have constructed for your costumes."

Irene, of course, was Thomas Smythe, James's partner on and off the stage.

"I've seen them," Niall said, moving to clap James's shoulder. "You're all going to adore them." And there was a fair chance none of the cast members would want to give their costumes back after the performance.

The cast began to filter out of the parlor and into the hall. The blast of cold air that wafted down the hall hinted that someone had already opened the front door.

"Now remember," Blake called over the din of the

JUST A LITTLE CHRISTMAS

departing cast as he stepped away from the piano, "Officer Murdoch could still be out there. We need everyone to be as vigilant as possible until Lord Clerkenwell can get the whole situation sorted within Scotland Yard."

"I'll sort the situation for you," one of the tougher men said from somewhere in the sea of the cast as Niall wedged his way into the hall. The others laughed. As long as they took the threat seriously, they could laugh as much as they wanted.

"Frances, you couldn't sort a deck of cards if there were only two left," Lionel's voice sounded from near the door.

Niall's brow went up as he spotted not only Lionel coming into the house, but Greta and her friend Katie with her. The hopes Niall had for a bit of "extra rehearsal" with Blake before the girls came home were dashed. He reminded himself not to be resentful of Blake's family. It was his family now too, after all, and he rather enjoyed being part of a family.

"Darling, what are you doing home so soon?" Blake asked as he, too, squeezed into the hall. It was filled with men putting on coats and hats and generally getting in each other's way as they left the rehearsal.

Greta and Katie were small enough to duck and dodge through the legs and skirts, but they didn't veer to the parlor whose doorway Niall and Blake stood in.

"String, Papa," Greta called out as she darted past

him and up the stairs, Katie in tow. "We need the string Xavier got at the store."

Niall didn't have the slightest idea what Greta was talking about. Neither he nor Blake tried to stop the girls, but Niall turned to Lionel—who was being buffeted left and right as he stood in front of the doorway—with an arched eyebrow.

"I know nothing at all about anything," Lionel said, clearly lying through his teeth. "I merely offered to escort the minxes here so that the Big Bad Wolf didn't snatch them up."

Blake's eyes narrowed, and he tensed by Niall's side. "Is Officer Murdoch back already?"

"Not yet," Lionel said, stepping forward as the last of the cast finally made it out the door. The relative quiet that followed was a bizarre contrast to how noisy the house had been all afternoon. "But that isn't good news," Lionel went on. "Apparently, Murdoch has friends now."

Niall's chest tightened. "Tell me that's a lie," he said in a somber voice.

Lionel shook his head. "I wish it were." The fact that he was so serious worried Niall. Lionel Mercer was only serious when there was something to be serious about. "We all knew it was only a matter of time before he convinced someone else in his godforsaken band of enforcers to meddle in our affairs along with him."

"Has anyone heard back from Lord Clerkenwell about calling them off?" Blake asked.

"Only that he has channels he has to go through to

JUST A LITTLE CHRISTMAS

have Murdoch reassigned and that declaring Darlington Gardens off-limits would do more harm than good." Lionel shrugged. "He agrees that we need to draw as little attention to ourselves as possible."

"Then it's nothing but a waiting game," Blake sighed, scrubbing a hand through his curly hair. He'd let it get too long in the past few weeks, but Niall had discovered he rather liked it. It gave him something to hold onto.

That thought had his mouth twitching into a grin that he should have saved for when the two of them were alone. Lionel was far too clever to miss a grin like that or to interpret it as something innocent.

Niall was saved the irritation of having to pretend he wasn't eager to get Blake alone as soon as possible when Greta and Katie came tearing back down the stairs once more, making enough racket for a dozen girls.

"Found it," Greta declared, holding up a skein of silver twine. "This will be perfect for the stars."

"Stars?" Blake shrugged and shook his head. "What stars?"

"What you don't know won't hurt you," Lionel said, back to only pretending to be serious again. He touched a pale, slender finger to the side of his nose.

"Are you girls causing trouble?" Blake asked, ever the father, following Greta and Katie to the doorway as they burst out into the cold street.

"I can assure you, we are causing all sorts of trouble," Lionel informed him, glancing briefly to Niall, then

81

rushing after the girls. "And we'll be causing it until at least five o'clock." He grinned cheekily.

"Now what do you suppose he meant by that?" Blake asked with a slight frown, shutting the front door and blocking out the cold.

Niall sauntered up to him, slipping his hands under Blake's jacket and waistcoat and along the warmth of his sides against his shirt. "I think it's pretty obvious what he meant," he said, then closed his mouth over Blake's.

Blake hummed, and laughed, as Niall pressed his back against the door and slipped his tongue into his mouth. It made Niall giddy to know they could fall into casual sexuality whenever they wanted to, and that he could devour Blake's mouth and fiddle with the fastenings of his trousers in the middle of the afternoon without anyone caring one whit. The mighty Duke of Selby went positively limp—except for the part of him that Niall reached into his trousers to stroke—the moment Niall made the slightest advance. He hadn't expected them to fall into such defined roles once their romance was rekindled. He'd always assumed they would be versatile, and maybe they would be again someday. But at the moment, nothing fired both of their blood faster than Niall being dominant and Blake surrendering to him.

"I was actually referring to what trouble Lionel and the girls were causing," Blake panted once Niall let him up for air, looping his arms over Niall's shoulders. "But I think I like your interpretation better."

Niall laughed, drawing his hand out of Blake's

JUST A LITTLE CHRISTMAS

trousers and leaning his forehead against Blake's for a moment as the tension pulsing through him lessened slightly. Their life was mad and sweet, and though not everything that needed to be resolved was yet, it was bursting with joy.

"What do you suppose Officer Murdoch would think if he could see through this door?" he asked against Blake's mouth before nipping Blake's bottom lip and sucking it into his mouth. That led naturally into a kiss of such intensity that involved lips and tongues and teeth and had Niall's cock straining against his trousers. Niall loved every sensual moment of it. He could spend his life kissing Blake and never grow tired of it.

"I think you'd better take me upstairs," Blake panted as soon as he could, clutching at Niall's shirt and pulling it out of his trousers as he did.

"I think that's a wise idea."

Niall pushed back, grabbing Blake's hand and sending him a wicked smile that promised every sort of unspeakable act of sensuality they could imagine before turning and leading him down the hall and up the stairs.

"Let's all move to London, he said," Blake laughed as they tore up the stairs, turning at the top to march on to their bedroom. "It'll be so much cozier than Yorkshire, he said. We'll be able to cohabitate without anyone being any wiser."

"I was right, wasn't I?" Niall turned on him as soon as they crossed into their room and shut the door behind them, the lock he'd had installed giving a satisfying click as he turned it. He spun back to face Blake, reaching for him.

Blake was already unbuttoning his jacket and waistcoat and loosening his necktie. "I never should have doubted you," he said, heat crackling in his hazel eyes.

Niall toed off his shoes and tore through the buttons of his waistcoat and shirt, desperate to be naked as fast as possible. "You doubted me?" He arched one eyebrow.

"I come from a world where there's a proper place for everything and everything should be in its proper place," Blake defended himself, shedding his clothes as he backed toward the bed.

"As far as I'm concerned, your proper place is under me and your prick's proper place is in my mouth, and I intend to enforce those proper places forthwith," Niall replied.

Blake laughed and stumbled as the back of his legs hit the edge of the bed. Niall's heart squeezed with fondness at the pure excitement in his lover's expression, as though every time between them were the first time and every kiss, every touch was new. He peeled off his trousers and socks as quickly as he could, thrilled that Blake was in an equal hurry to undress, then tumbled across the bed with him as soon as they were both naked.

He didn't hesitate for a moment before shifting Blake exactly the way he wanted him, as ridiculous as the splayed position, with Blake folded almost double, might have looked to an outsider. It brought them into intimate

JUST A LITTLE CHRISTMAS

contact in every way that mattered and allowed him to grind his cock and balls against Blake's.

"God, that feels good," Blake sighed, reaching to grasp the sides of Niall's head and pulling him down for a searing kiss.

It wasn't the most graceful Niall had ever been, but what he lacked in form he made up for in passion. He devoured Blake's mouth as though it were manna in the wilderness, invading with his tongue and bruising Blake's lips until Blake was groaning in surrender under him.

"And if you're very good," Niall teased, as though he were talking to a green lad instead of the man whose body he knew as well as his own, "Father Christmas will bring you something special this year."

"Father Christmas can give me whatever he wants," Blake replied with a naughty grin, tilting his hips up in a way that stimulated them both.

Niall sucked in a breath and lifted himself above Blake, sending him a stern look. "I positively draw the line at playing the role of Father Christmas while we fuck."

Blake laughed, the sound conveying pure happiness. "But I can think of so many metaphors involving peppermint sticks and stuffing stockings."

Niall dropped his head, laughing, and shook it. "I'll stuff your stocking, all right. And as for peppermint sticks...."

He slid down Blake's body, trailing kisses across his chest and belly until he reached the hot spear of Blake's cock resting hard against his abdomen. He reached for its base, holding it up so that he could lick it like a candy cane. Blake let out an impassioned sound of pleasure as he did and gripped the ornate brass-work of the bedstead behind him. That simple movement sent a jolt of lust through Niall as images of tying Blake to the bedstead and playing with forms of pleasure that they hadn't tried yet flashed into his imagination. There would be a time for everything, but at the moment, all he wanted to concentrate on was the salty taste of Blake's cock, the pre-cum he licked off its tip, and the way Blake gasped and shuddered as he did.

Niall's control was unraveling as fast as Blake's, but he still took the time to draw Blake fully into his mouth, swallowing him as deeply as he dared, then pushing himself to take more, over and over. His efforts were rewarded as Blake's sounds pitched higher and louder as he jerked reflexively into Niall's mouth, then cried out as he came. A rush of triumph and satisfaction warmed Niall as he swallowed, then pulled up for breath, continuing to stroke Blake's prick gently as he kissed his way back up his chest to Blake's neck and mouth.

"I don't even know—" Blake started in a happy, breathless voice before Niall cut him off with a kiss.

His blood was still on fire, and he was so aroused from Blake's taste and his reactions that the urgency pounding through him demanded immediate release. He didn't even want to waste time fishing for the jar of lubricant on the bedside table. Instead, he grabbed Blake's

JUST A LITTLE CHRISTMAS

hand and moved it to his throbbing cock, then thrust against him. Blake knew exactly what he wanted and fondled him deftly, grabbing his arse with his free hand. Niall kept their mouths together as long as he could before the desperation and abandon became too much. He came with a sharp cry, spilling across Blake's hand and wrist and losing himself in every last bit of the pleasure of the moment.

The contentment that washed over him as he dropped to Blake's side, stunned and satisfied, and let Blake wrap him in his arms, was the single most joyful thing he'd ever felt. He'd spent too long without Blake in the decade they'd been parted, and every moment of pleasure they shared now felt like it was making up for lost time.

Of course, when Blake teased him with, "Is that the best you can do?" Niall's eyes popped wide.

He blinked at Blake with mock incredulity. "Are you complaining?" he panted. "After the way I made you scream?"

"That was hardly a scream," Blake scoffed, shifting to rest his head against Niall's shoulder as he traced circles around one of Niall's nipples. "And besides," he glanced past Niall to the clock on their mantel, "it's not even three o'clock yet. We have two more hours until Lionel is finished leading the girls astray."

Niall's brow inched up as he, too, glanced to the clock. "In that case, give me about fifteen minutes to rest, and Father Christmas will show you how to really stuff a stocking."

Blake burst into laughter and hid his face against Niall's neck. Niall beamed up at the ceiling, laughing along with him. He didn't need some mythical benefactor to bring him joy and gifts for Christmas. He had everything he needed right there with him.

CHAPTER 7

David's caseload was exceptionally full for the Christmas season, though that didn't stop him from bringing his work to the ballroom of Danny and Phoebe's house and spreading out across a table in the back corner while Lionel directed the girls from Stephen and Max's orphanage, Blake's daughters, and a few random children that he had no idea where they'd come from, in rehearsal. Lionel led them through a dance he'd made up to accompany the song they would sing to surprise the adults at the upcoming Christmas party. David was supposed to be a solicitor, and the newly christened offices of Wirth & Mercer ostensibly handled legal cases of a variety of natures, but ever since word of his part in foiling the kidnapping ring led by three extremely highly-placed noblemen, everyone from members of The Brotherhood to random noblewomen who believed they'd

MERRY FARMER

been wronged in some way had crowded David and Lionel's office looking for help.

"That's it, Ursula," Lionel praised one of the girls as she imitated the pirouette he'd just completed. "Very lovely, darling. You make a perfect, pretend angel. Of course, we all know the truth that you're nothing more than an impish devil, but you are a graceful one."

The girls all giggled and blushed, watching Lionel with adoring eyes. David shook his head and paused to lean his chin on his hand as his elbow propped on one of the law books he'd been poring over. He knew damn well he was blushing too, and that he was just as besotted as Lionel's admirers. Lionel had never had trouble convincing people to worship him, but a marked change had come over the man in the past few months, since the two of them had had it out—in more ways than one. Lionel had confessed his fears that he was ill, and the two of them had pledged themselves to each other. It was almost paradoxical that breaking Lionel's fear-induced vow of celibacy—something they did on a daily basis— and indulging, safely, as much as they pleased had actually made Lionel behave less like a randy whore in public. He was now the favorite of children, for Christ's sake. Then again, David had always felt that Lionel's overt sexuality had an edge of desperation to it before, and now he was safe and taken care of in every way.

"Don't let every Tom, Dick, and Harry out in the street see you looking at him like that," the commanding voice of Jack Craig, Lord Clerkenwell, sounded suddenly

JUST A LITTLE CHRISTMAS

from the side of David's table. David jerked straight, his face going even hotter. Jack grinned at him. "You look like a lovesick schoolboy."

"Don't say that to Lionel," David replied with a mock wary look. "He'll never let me live it down. And besides, the entire point of Darlington Gardens is so that we can make utter fools of ourselves over our lovers without the fear of ending up in the pillory."

Jack chuckled and shrugged. "They did away with the pillory decades ago."

"But you never know when they'll bring something like that back," David said seriously, standing and moving to shake Jack's hand, which he felt he should have done immediately.

Jack made a noncommittal noise. "Your sort has made leaps and strides toward legitimacy in the last few decades," he argued. "Your way of loving is no longer punishable by death, after all."

David laughed humorlessly. "Tell that to the men who land in prison, sentenced to three years of hard labor under the Labouchere Amendment."

"That was a travesty of justice, I'll give you that," Jack sighed. "But word has it that even Labouchere himself didn't anticipate the way that clause would be used to persecute men like you."

"Yes, well, as I well know, the law often has unanticipated consequences," David grumbled. "Particularly when it falls into the hands of a zealous few who believe it is their right to meddle in other people's lives. We can

MERRY FARMER

barely walk from here to there in London without being accosted by one of these accursed blackmailers attempting to entrap us so that the papers can have a new, sordid headline."

"All the same," Jack argued on, "I have it on good authority that only a tiny fraction of men who are arrested are actually prosecuted, and of those, an infinitesimal number of rulings go against the men who are accused. So you cannot draw conclusions about the attitudes of society toward your sort based on numbers of arrests alone."

David stared at Jack, his brow shooting up, though he wasn't sure whether he was angry with the man for his glib attitude toward even the few who landed in real trouble, or pleased to know that very little ever came of the arrests that were made besides personal embarrassment. "Whether every arrest that results from some bigot's suspicion of what we do behind closed doors leads to a prison term or not, the fact is that our sort live with a constant cloud hanging over our heads. Yes, attitudes might have been indifferent for any number of decades, but thanks to the Cleveland Street scandal last year, the tide is turning against us once more. I fear the freedom of anonymity that we've had for years now could be crushed by just one more high-profile case. The more so-called ordinary people are aware of us, the more dangerous our lives become. And I fear it will continue to be this way unless and until public attitudes become completely the opposite of what they are now.

JUST A LITTLE CHRISTMAS

And how long will that take? A decade? A century? Forever?"

David knew he was becoming too worked up over his thoughts and concerns, but the way Jack clapped a hand to his shoulder to steady him, and the sympathetic look in the man's eyes made him feel downright sheepish for becoming so impassioned for his cause.

"Attitudes will change, my friend," Jack said, then added, "Though I fear that change will come slowly. Particularly when you have ignoramuses, like Officer Murdoch, running around with an inferiority complex born out of jealousy over someone different living a better, happier life."

David sighed and rubbed a hand over his face, glancing sideways at Lionel and the girls before facing Jack again. "I take it you've found out more about our friend, Officer Murdoch, and his intentions."

Lionel had definitely noticed Jack's arrival, and though he was still leading the girls through their ballet, he watched David and Jack intently. As far as David was concerned, there was little point in Jack explaining things to just him when he would have to repeat himself for Lionel, so he waved for Lionel to end what he was doing and join the conversation.

Lionel nodded slightly, his expression grave for a moment, before he put on a bright smile and turned to the girls. "Very good, my lovely little demons. And now I think it's time for us to take a break. Besides, I need someone to devour this bag of gumdrops for me."

MERRY FARMER

He pulled a fat bag of colorful gumdrops from his pocket—the amount of money Lionel spent on sweets for the girls these days was downright ludicrous to David—and dropped it into the hands of the first girl to race to his side. The girls all burst into shrieks and giggles as they chased the girl with the bag across the room, nearly upsetting a few pieces of furniture and bunching up one end of the oriental carpet as they did. Lionel brushed his hands as though he were done with the whole thing and headed over to join David and Jack.

"Lord Clerkenwell." He greeted Jack with an outstretched hand, his mannerisms more fey than usual. "How delicious to see you this afternoon."

David crossed his arms and rolled his eyes, even though his heart danced with fondness. The only time Lionel behaved so ridiculously toward a man who wasn't like them was when he felt like his position as the most powerful man in the room was threatened. And while it was true that Lionel had enough power to command an army with a single crook of his finger, one could argue that Jack Craig was one of the few men in London who could out-command him.

"Mr. Mercer." Jack shook Lionel's hand with a twitch of his mouth that said he knew exactly what game Lionel was playing.

Judging by how white both men's knuckles went during the handshake, they were attempting to out-muscle each other too. David had to hide his grin with

94

JUST A LITTLE CHRISTMAS

one hand. It would take him the rest of the day to soothe and stroke Lionel's ego after the impending conversation.

"So what have you learned about Officer Murdoch?" David asked, hoping to push things along.

"He's a boob," Jack growled.

He looked as though he'd wanted to use a much stronger word, but the giggling pack of girls had finished their race for gumdrops nearby. They'd all collapsed to sit on the floor, chewing stickily and keeping an eye on Lionel, to see if he had some other trick up his sleeve, no doubt.

Jack went on. "The man has no special talent and below average intelligence. There are too many like him at the Met, if you ask me. What he lacks in ability, he's trying to make up for in causing a sensation. He, and every other boob like him, took note of the sensationalism the Cleveland Street scandal caused last year, and he's been bragging that he can get his name in the papers, just like the officers involved in that case did."

"So the man is looking for fame at our expense," David grumbled, his brow knitting into a dark frown in spite of the fact that he knew he had a face that could frighten children when he was upset.

"It appears so," Jack sighed.

"And what can be done about it?" Lionel asked with false serenity. David was well aware of the ferocity in his eyes. He caught the protective look Lionel sent the girls— who seemed far more interested than they should in the

MERRY FARMER

adults' conversation, particularly Blake's daughters, Jane, and Katie—and the hard set of Lionel's jaw.

"I'm attempting to have Murdoch reassigned," Jack said with a sigh. "But he's not technically under my jurisdiction."

"You're an assistant commissioner," David said. "I thought everything was under your jurisdiction."

"Yes and no." Jack rubbed his chin and scowled. "When one reaches as lofty a height as I'm at, everything is at your disposal, but nothing is under your control. Which, I'm certain, is exactly what my father-in-law wanted."

David sent the man a sympathetic smile. It was an open secret that Jack had been given his towering position in the Metropolitan Police and his title by his extraordinarily powerful father-in-law, Lord Malcolm Campbell, in order to make him worthy of marrying Lord Campbell's daughter, who, as it turned out, he'd already impregnated. David found the whole story amusing, but then, he hadn't had to live through having his life twisted beyond recognition so that he could marry the love of his life. No, he was merely legally prevented from marrying the love of his life and forced to sell a perfectly good house and move to a secluded square—one that was now under threat of raid by a man with a small brain who probably wouldn't know true love if it bit him in the arse —so that he could live with Lionel.

"And so, I repeat," Lionel said overdramatically, "what can be done to prevent a lout like Murdoch from

JUST A LITTLE CHRISTMAS

destroying the lives we have all so carefully and clandestinely constructed for ourselves? Because my darling husband and I have only just moved to this square, and we would rather like to live a long and happy life here together instead of ending up on trial for gross indecency in the new year." Lionel leaned into David's side, taking his hand and holding it tightly.

David clenched his jaw and forced himself not to flinch or be angry with Lionel. Instinct told him Lionel was a damned fool for calling him husband in front of Jack and the girls, but another part of him knew that Lionel was far braver than him for speaking the truth proudly and openly.

Jack glanced between David and Lionel as more of the girls finished their gumdrops and looked on, as though watching a play. "You've got the right idea by setting up a community patrol, of sorts," he said. "I would send men from the Met to help, but I fear doing so would only draw attention. As I mentioned earlier, I'm working to have Murdoch reassigned—and I hope that I'll be able to spread the word as quietly as possible not to bother Darlington Gardens—but everything takes time, and matters that are particularly delicate take even more time."

"I think you will find, Lord Clerkenwell, that while we may appear delicate," Lionel began with a soft and coy demeanor, then switched to a look and stance as hard as iron and as masculine as any prize fighter, "we are not."

"Understood, Mr. Mercer." Jack nodded.

"I hate being called delicate," Jane said, leaping to her feet and stomping over to join the conversation.

David's mouth pulled into a lopsided grin at the proof that the girls were listening in, but he had to hand it to Jane. She was as tough as nails under her frilly pinafore and hair ribbons.

He was even more delighted when the rest of the girls popped up—one by one at first, then in a mass—and formed a veritable battalion as they stood before him, Lionel, and Jack.

"This is our home," Katie said, planting her fists on her hips. Many of the other girls imitated her posture. "Officer Murdoch has no right to behave badly in our home."

"He keeps coming around and making eyes at Miss Flora," a girl who David thought was named Ivy complained.

"He doesn't know that Miss Flora is actually Mr. Tarleton," one of the older girls who had been rescued from the kidnapping ring over the summer, Hattie, added with a snort.

"Mr. Tarleton is only nice to him so he won't bother everyone else," Blake's daughter, Greta said.

David's brow inched up. The observation was rather astute for a nine-year-old. It made him wonder what other astute observations the girls of Darlington Gardens had made, which made him suddenly come over hot and cold and prickly with awkwardness. He loosened his grip on Lionel's hand, but Lionel wouldn't let him drop it.

JUST A LITTLE CHRISTMAS

"I told you they were a pack of little devils," Lionel whispered to him instead. "Never underestimate the observations of children. They might not know how to interpret what they see, but they see everything."

"Something tells me truer words were never spoken," David murmured back.

"Sir always says we should go to police officers if we ever need help," a girl David thought was called Lottie said. The others turned to her, some nodding. "He says they are here to keep us safe and to protect us from bad people."

"Most of them are," David assured her. "Lord Clerkenwell is the boss of the police officers, and I'm sure he'd agree."

"It's true." Jack smiled fondly at the girls. He had several children of his own and knew how to talk to them. "Every single one of the police officers working for Her Majesty have sworn to keep you safe."

"But what about Officer Murdoch?" Jane crossed her arms and narrowed her eyes at Jack, as though she wasn't afraid even of the boss of all police officers. "He's trying to harm us all."

Several of the other girls agreed with Jane, crossing their arms and challenging Jack as well.

"The problem is, Officer Murdoch thinks he's doing his job," Jack explained. "He is mistaken, though, and he will be corrected soon."

Jane didn't look satisfied with the answer. Neither did most of the rest of the girls.

MERRY FARMER

"I'm not going to let anyone, even if he's a police officer, harm my friends or my Papa or Niall," Jessie, Blake's younger daughter, said with a fierce light in her eyes. "The grown-ups take turns watching us, and I think we should take turns watching them."

"Yes, we should," several of the other girls agreed.

"This is our home too," Ivy added.

"I don't want anyone interfering with our home," Katie said.

The girls rang out in a chorus of agreement that had David blinking and staring at them, brow raised. "I think we're about to have a mutiny on our hands," he murmured to Lionel.

"Not a mutiny, love," Lionel said, beaming with pride, a mischievous light of approval in his eyes that would likely land the lot of them in serious trouble. "This is a revolution."

"I have an idea," Greta declared over the buzz of the girls' conversation. "We need to—" She stopped, mouth hanging open, and glanced warily to Jack, then on to David and Lionel. From there, she closed her mouth, cleared her throat, and turned to the three men with a suddenly sweet smile. "If you please, sirs, we would like to have a conversation alone." She glanced to the rest of her sisters-in-arms.

David was so stunned over being dismissed by a nine-year-old that be burst into a smile and nearly laughed out loud. That would have severely hurt the girls' pride, though, so he bit his tongue.

JUST A LITTLE CHRISTMAS

"By all means," Lionel said, far better at feigning absolute seriousness and respect. "We'll just take ourselves over to the far corner of the room and allow you to plot your domination over by the piano." He gestured to the far corner of the room.

"Good idea," Katie said, nodded, then tore off to the other side of the room. The rabble of little girls followed her.

"Are you sure it's wise to let them get into trouble like that?" Jack asked as he, David, and Lionel retreated to their end of the room.

"You saw the looks in their eyes," Lionel said. "They're going to plan something no matter what we do."

"At least this way, we'll still be able to keep an eye on them without them being any the wiser," David said, catching on to Lionel's logic.

"They have as much a right as anyone to defend their home," Lionel went on, growing more serious. "And remember, most of those girls are orphans. They were cast off and abandoned to Stephen at best. At worst, they were kidnapped from their homes and put through unspeakable tortures before being rescued this summer. Here, with Stephen and Max and the gentlemen of Darlington Gardens, they have known peace and family and home for the first time in their lives. This place is as much a haven for them as it is for the rest of us, and as far as I'm concerned, they have earned the right to protect it with their whole hearts if they want to."

"Well, when you put it like that," Jack said, shoulders

MERRY FARMER

dropping as he let out a breath. He smiled, though there were equal parts sadness and regret in the look. "I suddenly feel the need to go home and embrace my wife and children."

"And I feel the need to supply those girls with whatever weapons they ask for," David said, a strange mix of pride, love, and unspeakable agony filling his heart. As unfair as the world had been to men like him, it was equally unfair for children, especially girls, especially those born in poverty. He reached for Lionel's hand twining their fingers together and squeezing. Now he understood why Lionel was so devoted to the girls. They had far more in common than any outsider would ever guess, and David was just as determined to give his all for them now as anyone.

CHAPTER 8

For a man who had been ignominiously disowned by his family and was about to spend his first Christmas without so much as a card from anyone whose surname he shared, Maxwell Hillsboro was extraordinarily happy.

"Mercy, put that book down and blow your candle out," he told one of the girls as he made his rounds through the upper floor of dormitory rooms. "Sarah, give Hattie her blanket back. If you need another one, we have plenty in the linen closet. Jane, darling, what in heavens name is that under your pillow."

"Nothing!" Jane yelped and shoved whatever it was deeper into the pillow.

Max arched one eyebrow and crossed his arms, pretending to be put out by her mischievousness, though, in fact, he found Jane to be adorable and as sharp as a

MERRY FARMER

whip. He marched over to her bed and gave her a questioning look.

"Honestly, Max, it's nothing. I swear," Jane insisted, as guilty as sin.

Max held out his hand, gesturing for her to give him whatever she was hiding. Jane heaved a dramatic sigh and grumbled as she took a stick as thick as her wrist out from under her pillow. She handed it to Max with a sullen scowl.

Max's mouth twitched into an amused grin. "What in heaven's name is this?"

"It's a stick." Jane blinked dumbly up at him. It was an act, of course, but Max couldn't figure out for the life of him why Jane would be sleeping with such a thing under her pillow.

"What's this on the end?" he asked, taking a closer look. One end of the stick looked as though she'd been trying to whittle it into...into something.

"I—I was going to carve it into a snake." Jane's eyes filled with inspiration. "Yes, that's what I was going to do. It's a new project."

Max narrowed his eyes and turned the stick over. On the one hand, the girls of his and Stephen's orphanage had been trying their hand at every sort of skill and craft imaginable, thanks to the efforts of the residents of Darlington Gardens. Everyone in the square wanted to share what they knew with the girls in an effort to help them gain skills they could use for gainful employment in the future. The

JUST A LITTLE CHRISTMAS

girls had been trying their hands at everything from painting to music to sewing, which was lovely, but they'd also been learning carpentry, bookkeeping, accounting, and other skills that, while highly useful, weren't exactly profes sions women took part in. Whittling was new, though.

"It can't be comfortable to sleep with this under your pillow," he said, handing the stick back to Jane.

"It...it helps me to think better," she said, looking shocked at her excuse.

Max eyed her suspiciously, letting her know he wasn't fooled for a moment. A few of the other girls giggled and dove under their covers, looking as if they knew something Max didn't. In fact, the more he glanced around the room, the clearer it was to him that the girls were plotting something. Then again, Christmas was in two days, and everyone reserved the right to have secrets at Christmas.

"The lot of you'd better not be planning something naughty," he said, turning to address all six of the girls who shared the room. There was more space in the new orphanage than there had been in the old one, but more space meant they could create a home for more girls, so rooms still had to be shared and packed to capacity. "Father Christmas will be coming tomorrow night, and I have it on good authority he only brings sweets and presents to good girls."

"We're all good girls," Hattie argued. "Just you wait and see."

MERRY FARMER

"Hattie, shush!" Sarah hissed. "It's supposed to be a surprise."

Max's brow flew up. So the girls were plotting something after all.

He tried to hide his grin, but his love for his and Stephen's charges was just too much. He might have lost one high and mighty, aristocratic family, but he'd gained a whole different, far more precious family in the process.

"All right, now," he said, making a final round of the room to tuck girls in and kiss their foreheads. "Enough silliness for one day. Go to sleep and dream of sugar plums and—"

He stopped as his foot hit something tucked halfway under Mercy's bed. With a curious frown, he bent all the way to see what it was. He could feel the girls all holding their breaths and inching up to stare at him with wide, worried eyes as he pulled a small crate of pine cones from under the bed.

"Pine cones?" he asked Mercy, holding up the box.

"I—I've decided to collect them," Mercy said, her eyes wide.

It was a bald-faced lie, he could tell, but following on his previous thought, it *was* Christmas, and pine cones could be used in any number of crafty projects.

"I see," he said, putting the crate back where he'd found it. As he did, he noticed a second box with sticks in it. Unlike Jane's sticks, the ones in Mercy's box were all forked, though they were still sturdy. He decided not to comment on it. They were probably for decorations

106

JUST A LITTLE CHRISTMAS

anyhow. "Well, good night." He kissed Mercy's forehead, then headed toward the door. "Sweet dreams, loves."

"Sweet dreams, Max," a small chorus replied.

Max grinned from ear to ear as he turned off the electric lights and shut the door. Any outside observer who had been privy to his life just a year ago would say that he'd fallen far and hard. His family had stricken his name from their Bible—even though his father and brother George were the ones who had been humiliated after their arrest and imprisonment in connection with the kidnapping ring—and no one in high society so much as whispered his name anymore, let alone invited him to gatherings and events. He'd even given up using his title and had David looking into ways he could renounce the damn thing officially. And as mad as it was, as big of a target as it might paint on his forehead, he was actually contemplating legally changing his surname to Siddel as a gift to Stephen. The world could curse him as the worst sort of reprobate, but he knew the truth of things. He was blessed in ways most people couldn't possibly comprehend.

"Katie, why on earth is there a box of rocks in your wardrobe?" Stephen's voice sounded from the room near the stairs just as Max was about to head down to his and Stephen's room to retire for the night. The question sparked Max's own suspicions, so he changed course and popped his head into the room.

"A box of rocks?" he asked, staring straight at Katie.

"They're for...for a project," Katie insisted, then drew

her blanket up to her eyes as if hiding a grin she couldn't suppress.

"What sort of project requires a box of rocks?" Stephen asked from the open wardrobe door, puzzling over the hatbox in his hands.

"They're up to something," Max said, unable to hide his feelings or the mischief that came with them when Stephen glanced his way. "The little wenches are plotting behind our backs," he went on with a smile. He winked at Stephen, then turned his grin on the girls.

There were five girls in Katie's room, and all of them giggled and looked as guilty as sin as they snuggled into their beds.

"Plotting?" Stephen pretended disapproval as he put the box of rocks away and shut the wardrobe door, then went from bed to bed, tucking girls in and kissing their cheeks. "Does Father Christmas know about this plotting?"

"We all know that *you* are Father Christmas, Sir," Katie said when he reached her. "*We're* not babies," she said in a tone that implied other girls at the orphanage were.

"We'll just see about that," Stephen said with a wink, then kissed her cheek. "No more plotting tonight," he said as he joined Max in the doorway. "Only sleeping. Is that clear?"

"Yes, Sir," the girls replied.

"Good night and sweet dreams, then."

JUST A LITTLE CHRISTMAS

"Sweet dreams, Sir, Max," the girls replied in a jumble of words, snuggling into their beds.

Stephen turned out the lights and stepped out into the hall with Max, shutting the door. "They're up to no good," he said, sparks of fondness in his eyes.

"Oh, of course they are," Max replied, sliding his arms around Stephen and leaning into him. "Aren't we all?"

Stephen sent Max a teasing look, his mouth twitching into a wry grin, and rested his hands on Max's hips. "I swear, you're as bad as the lot of them."

"No, I'm considerably worse," Max replied, lowering his voice to a purr and leaning in to kiss Stephen.

Kissing Stephen freely, whenever he wanted, was one of the greatest joys of his new life. He knew Stephen's mouth—and the rest of him—so well now, knew exactly how much Stephen loved the swipe of his tongue and the way he nibbled on his lower lip before deepening things with a contented sigh. His father would likely die of apoplexy if he knew half the things that he and Stephen did with impunity, not caring who in their protected home saw them.

He and Stephen had tried concealing their relationship from the girls in the orphanage at first, but that hadn't made it past the first month after they'd moved to Darlington Gardens. They were glaringly obvious in their affection, for one. The looks and touches they shared could have been explained away or dismissed, but their clever girls had been quick to realize no one actually slept in the room that was supposedly Max's, and that he and Stephen, in fact, shared the same room. With only one bed in it. Max had been terrified of how the girls would react to the scandalous revelation, and indeed, it had caused a stir at first. But the minds of children were malleable and forgiving. Mrs. Ross had advised them to act as though nothing were out of the ordinary, and within days, a new normal had been established. Although, it helped that everyone else in the square was of the same mind. Max's only worry now was what their girls would say when they set out to make their own ways in the world.

"If you're going to start with that, you'd better take yourselves downstairs," Mrs. Ross said as she headed up the stairs, a covered plate in her hands, spotting their amorous embrace.

Max pulled away from kissing Stephen, but stayed in his arms. "You don't know what the girls are plotting, do you, Mrs. Ross?" he asked. Yes, the world Max lived in now was absolutely a different one if he barely batted an eyelash when someone caught him with his lips locked on Stephen's.

Mrs. Ross laughed as she turned the corner at the top of the stairs. "They're girls. They're up to anything and everything."

"They seem to be up to something specific this time," Max said.

"Lionel has taught them a song to sing at the Christmas party tomorrow," Stephen informed him.

JUST A LITTLE CHRISTMAS

Max twisted to raise his eyebrows at Stephen in surprise. "And you didn't tell me?"

"I only just found out myself," Stephen laughed. "Blake wheedled the truth out of his girls and promised not to tell."

"So much for *that* promise," Mrs. Ross snorted a laugh and shook her head. "Men. You can't keep secrets to save your lives."

"I think the very fact that we're all here proves that we can keep secrets, especially when they save our lives," Stephen fired back at her.

Mrs. Ross winked at him. "I'll give you that one." She continued down the hall.

"What do you have there?" Max called after her, nodding to her plate.

Mrs. Ross paused to turn back to them, touching a finger to her lips in warning, then lifting the side of the cloth to reveal several mince pies on the plate. "I'm having my Christmas celebration tonight," she whispered.

"Christmas celebration?" Max grinned at her, then at Stephen.

"Mince pies," Mrs. Ross said with a wide grin, "a nice, hot bath in the fancy, newfangled tub Mr. Long so conveniently installed along with fancy, newfangled plumbing in all these houses, and the latest issue of *Nocturne* to keep me company."

Stephen laughed, "You're not keeping company with Mr. Norris, the baker, then?"

MERRY FARMER

Mrs. Ross laughed out loud. "Son, when you reach my age, mince pies and a warm bath are far more of a treat than even the tastiest sausage roll." She winked at them, then continued down the hall, chuckling at her own joke.

"Speak for yourself," Max purred, shifting to grab Stephen's hand. "I'm rather fond of a big, juicy sausage roll myself."

"A little too fond sometimes," Stephen laughed, letting himself be pulled downstairs.

As soon as they reached their bedroom one floor down, and shut and locked the door behind them, Max said, "There's no such thing as being *too* fond of sausage rolls."

He swayed seductively closer to Stephen, throwing his arms around Stephen's sides and bringing their mouths crashing together again.

It was perfect. Everything about the moment, the day they'd just had, the Christmas season they were in the middle of, and Max's life was sheer perfection. He had the man he loved in his arms, and aside from the lingering worries that Officer Murdoch represented—worries that had always existed and likely always would—they had somehow managed to create a wildly improbable haven for themselves. And yet, in spite of the uniqueness of Darlington Gardens, the last few months had proven to Max that, with enough support and camaraderie from their own kind, a life like theirs wasn't just probable, it was a given. Even if the rest of the world didn't suspect a thing.

"We should really take care of a bit of business before going to bed," Stephen said breathlessly between kisses, working open the buttons of Max's waistcoat and tugging his shirt out of his trousers. "We've the payroll to sort out and Christmas bonuses to divvy up for Mrs. Ross and Annie, the new cook, the maids, and the teachers."

"It can wait," Max hummed, nipping at Stephen's earlobe as he unfastened Stephen's trousers.

"And then there are the bills to pay," Stephen went on, his tone far too seductive for a man listing off work that needed to be done. "The butcher, the baker—"

"The candlestick maker?" Max finished for him, thrusting a hand into Stephen's trousers.

Stephen was hot and already hard as Max teased him. His cock was better than a candlestick any day. That was another part of Stephen that Max knew so well now. The heat and excitement of a new lover was one thing, but the carnal familiarity of a long-term lover, the soul-deep affection and devotion that came with commitment, was a thousand times better and increasing every day.

"I love you," he murmured against Stephen's mouth, kissing him again. "I can't say that enough. I love everything about you."

Stephen made a sound of acceptance and longing as he pushed Max's waistcoat and suspenders off his shoulders. They were forced apart for a moment as Stephen peeled Max's shirt off over his head, then yanked him close again by the band of his trousers before making quick work of those fastenings.

"And I love you," Stephen said, pushing Max's trousers and drawers to his thighs and grabbing handfuls of Max's arse as he did. He spread his cheeks and slipped a finger down to toy with his hole as he kissed Max again. "Every time I think I couldn't possibly love you more, I wake up in the morning and my love has doubled."

Max chuckled against Stephen's mouth. "That's not your love, that's your morning wood," he joked.

Stephen pulled back, a sly grin on his kiss-reddened lips, and slapped Max's backside. "Get ready for bed, you cheeky bastard." He shook his head and stepped to the side to set his glasses on the bedside table, then went to work undressing.

Max did as he was ordered, giddy expectation swirling through him. Never in a hundred years would he have thought the utilitarian acts of undressing, brushing his teeth, using what Mrs. Ross would call the fancy, newfangled toilet in the washroom attached to their bedroom, and doing half a dozen other mundane things could leave him so hot and ready for passion. He'd always imagined sex to be something furtive and wicked, stolen in the dark of night and never spoken of again. And while that sort of activity did have a naughty appeal to it, climbing into bed while his lover brushed his teeth and washed up in the other room, then waiting in domestic bliss, his hands under his head as he lay back against the pillow, watching the washroom door with anticipation, was surprisingly erotic. It promised permanence and security, that Stephen would always be with him, and that they would always satisfy each other.

"And now, about that sausage roll," Stephen said as he sauntered back into the room, prick already well on its way to standing at attention. He set his glasses on their bedside table and reached into the drawer to take out a jar of ointment to have at the ready. The casual gesture sent Max's blood pumping.

Stephen threw back the covers, gazing admiringly at Max's body as he nudged his knees aside and knelt between them. Max sat up, sliding his hands up Stephen's sides and repositioning himself to straddle Stephen's hips. Stephen gripped his backside, both for balance and to press their bodies together. The cold snap of the winter air was a sensual contrast to the heat of their bodies as they kissed.

"Have I mentioned that I love you?" Max asked with a mischievous grin.

Stephen rolled his eyes, though his cheeks burned pink and fire entered his eyes. "Have I mentioned you're a maudlin sap?"

"Perhaps once or twice." Max stroked his hands across Stephen's back, digging his fingertips into Stephen's muscles. He was a sap, and he was proud of it. But he was as much a man as anyone else, and the way Stephen wedged against him while spreading his arse wider and fingering him had him throbbing in no time.

Stephen's kisses turned fierce and demanding,

MERRY FARMER

leaving Max's heart thumping against his ribs and the tip of his cock slick with pre-cum. He couldn't help but reach between them to grasp their pricks together and work them both into a hot, panting frenzy.

"Are you in a hurry to finish?" Stephen said with a sigh. Max figured he was trying to be sarcastic, but they'd rocketed each other to the edge right out of the gate.

"I'm in a hurry to have you in me," Max replied, looking Stephen in the eye.

That eye contact was like throwing paraffin on a fire. "Turn around," Stephen whispered.

Max bit his lip and disengaged himself from Stephen enough to wriggle to face the bedstead as Stephen reached for the jar on the bedside table. They knew each other's rhythms and routines enough that Max knew it would be fast and hot and so, so good tonight. They knew what they wanted, and they knew exactly how to take care of each other.

Max gripped the bedstead, still on his knees, and arched his back. He sucked in a sharp breath as the cold slip of ointment accompanied Stephen's fingers in his hole. He let that breath out on a long, expressive sigh as Stephen pushed into him. The sensation was as familiar as breathing now, but even more pleasurable than Max could ever have dreamed of. Especially once Stephen eased himself all the way in until their thighs pressed against each other.

"You feel so good," Stephen gasped as he jerked

JUST A LITTLE CHRISTMAS

gently into Max to start out. He caressed Max's sides and chest, kissing and biting Max's shoulder as he did.

Max closed his eyes and made a sound of enjoyment as he moved in concert with Stephen. Nothing he could think of felt better. His body was both used to Stephen's and hungry for more, which Stephen gladly gave him. He started moving faster and thrusting harder, hitting just the right spot inside of Max. Max let out a sound of pleasure that would have shocked even the most seasoned whore. His knuckles went white on the bedstead as Stephen brought one hand down to his hip to hold Max steady, and the other closed over his throbbing cock. There was no way he would be able to hold out for long with every part of him alive with pleasure, but be breathed into it, accepting Stephen and vocalizing his pleasure as Stephen's body grew more and more tense around him.

They were both close, in rare synchronicity, when Stephen bit Max's shoulder, the plaintive sounds he made indicating he was transported. It was beautiful, sensual, and amazing, and Max celebrated everything it meant by coming hard in Stephen's hand. Stephen gasped and let out a cry mere moments later, jerking mercilessly into Max as he came, before his energy drained away. Max let go of the bedstead and let Stephen's weight and exhaustion draw him down into a satisfied tangle of sweaty, overheated bodies with him.

"I love you," Stephen panted, rolling to his back and bringing Max with him.

"So we're both saps for saying it so much," Max laughed, nestling against him, wedging his thigh between Stephen's legs.

"We're hopeless," Stephen mumbled happily, already falling asleep.

Max couldn't blame him. They'd become skilled in the art of wearing each other out. But if that was the worst anyone could say about him, Max would have it carved on his grave. A grave he fully intended to share with Stephen...but not for many decades to come.

CHAPTER 9

John Dandie was beginning to think it was a mistake to take a room above the office he'd rented for his new practice upon his return to London several months ago. Walking through Darlington Gardens on his way to the home of Danny and Phoebe Long for the Christmas party he'd somehow managed an invite to was like walking through a dream world. He shouldn't have been at all surprised that a square inhabited almost entirely by members of The Brotherhood would be decorated so magnificently. Not only were the wreaths hanging on the door of every house on the square coordinated in terms of size, shape, decorations, and ribbons, matching wreathes, garlands, and bows were hung all around the low wall bordering the park in the center of the square. Several of the trees inside the park were hung with silver baubles and ribbons as well. There were even candles burning in many of the windows of the houses facing the square, though John spotted people blowing them out as more and more residents of the square headed outside and along the road to the Longs' house. It was a wise move, all things considered. As he understood it, Darlington Gardens was too precious to its residents to risk a stray Christmas candle falling over and burning the whole place to the ground.

John smiled at all the thought and care that the residents showed their home, nodding and waving to a few men he knew as he made his final approach to the Longs' house at the far end of the square. The world he'd suddenly found himself in upon his return to London was vastly different from the one he'd left in Manchester that fall. He'd lived well in Manchester. His law office had been a success. He'd never lacked for clientele. He'd even managed to carry on a love affair or two, though none of them had lasted. The care he and his lovers had needed to take not to be discovered was as much of a strain as the benefits of a lover were a pleasure. London was a different place, though. It was well known to be, if not accepting of his sort, at least tolerant. As long as none of them made too much noise or lived too openly.

Only in London would a self-made man like Danny Long be able to pack his ballroom full of men—and a few women—who would have been arrested if they'd shown up in public looking the way they did for the Christmas party. John grinned and shook his head as he entered the buzzing ballroom and marveled at everything he saw. A stage was set up at the far end of the room with a band of

JUST A LITTLE CHRISTMAS

musicians tuning their instruments seated beside it. Blake sat at the piano next to the musicians, helping them tune, by the look of things. Niall stood immediately behind the piano bench, and though he was facing away from Blake as he chatted to a pair of gentlemen in costumes, the two were close enough that Blake could have leaned against Niall as a backrest.

The sight made John's heart feel light. He'd watched the two lovers fall apart at university, and now it seemed he would be able to watch them fall back together and live out the rest of their lives in peace and happiness. If he could work a bit of legal and investigative magic to find Ian Archibald, Annamarie, and Blake's son, Alan, then their happiness would be complete.

The lightness in his heart turned to steely determination. He would reunite Blake with his son and see to it personally that Blake received the divorce he deserved so that he and Niall and their family could live happily ever after. Nothing would stop him from seeing to it that justice was done. As he glanced around the cheery, festive room, enjoying the way it practically bubbled with excitement, he spotted someone who might just be able to help his case.

"Mr. Archibald." He nodded to Ian's brother, Edward Archibald, who currently served as an MP from York, as he approached the man.

Edward flinched at the sound of his name and shrank away from John, a look of alarm in his eyes, as though he'd been caught doing something he shouldn't. As soon

MERRY FARMER

as he recognized John, that alarm lessened, but only by a hair. "Dandie," he said straightening and offering his hand gingerly. "Good evening."

John didn't bother to hide his amused grin as he took Edward's hand, then shifted to thump his back and stand beside him, looking out at the party guests. "Don't worry, man," he said. "Nobody here is going to run to the press to alert them that a member of Parliament is attending a party full of poufs."

His teasing only made Edward blush and stammer, "I-I wasn't concerned about—" He pressed his lips shut and breathed out through his nose when John sent him a disbelieving sideways look. "I've a reputation to protect," he admitted sheepishly. "Can you imagine what the press would do if they found an MP in a place like this?"

John shrugged. "There are any number of prominent businessmen, lords, and public figures in attendance. Why, look over there." He pointed across the room to where the actors were assembling for the panto. "That's Everett Jewel in that lovely, sparkly costume with his face painted like a tart. And I have it on good authority that that's Martin Piper under that Father Christmas beard."

"Martin Piper?" Edward perked up, glancing across the room to where Martin was making a comedic show of handing out candy to the girls who crowded around him.

John arched one eyebrow, grinning over Edward's reaction.

Edward must have caught his curious look. "I-I frequent the theater," he said, blushing even harder. "It's

JUST A LITTLE CHRISTMAS

a relief to be able to sit in the dark without anyone knowing who I am sometimes. I've been enjoying Mr. Piper's performance in *Love's Last Lesson* this fall. He makes me laugh."

"Yes, Martin has a bright future in front of him as a comedic lead, or so Niall informs me," John said, though what he thought was, "I *bet* you've been enjoying his performance."

He didn't have time to tease poor, stodgy, timid Edward about it, though. Niall had started gathering the girls and directing them to sit in front of the stage, and the orchestra was finishing tuning as though the play would start at any moment.

"I've been meaning to ask you, Edward." John turned to him, growing more serious. "Do you know your brother Ian's whereabouts?"

Edward lost his anxious, hunted air as he frowned. "No, I do not," he admitted, looking every bit the serious politician he was. "He hasn't attempted to contact me at all since absconding with Lady Selby and Lord Stanley. But to be fair, we've never been particularly close."

"Understood." John rubbed his chin. "All the same, do you think that you could—"

He was prevented from asking Edward to take a more active part in the search for Ian as the orchestra burst into the opening notes of a song and Everett leapt onto the stage with a bow and arrow covered in some sort of glitter in his hands.

MERRY FARMER

"Oh, he's Robin Hood," Edward said, as though everything made sense now.

That was the last of the conversation they were able to have. When Everett Jewel was on stage, everyone in the room stopped what they were doing to watch him. If they didn't, Everett would have marched around the room slapping people until they did. John gestured for Edward to take a seat at the edge of the rows of chairs that had been set up for the show, but Edward declined, keeping to the shadows, as John assumed he was used to. John ended up sitting next to a devilishly handsome black man in a fine suit who he was reasonably certain was the renowned composer Samuel Percy, though the two of them had never been introduced.

"And now, my merry men," Everett belted from the stage once his song had ended, "let us leave Sherwood Forest to woo the saucy maidens of Nottingham."

John laughed and shook his head as half a dozen men in elaborate drag pranced onto the stage, led by an incredibly convincing Maid Marion. The girls—all of whom were seated at the front, watching with stars in their eyes, not realizing that what they were seeing would shock the sunshine out of half of the moralizing mamas of England —laughed uproariously at the improvised comedy of the silly maidens.

John leaned back in his chair, crossing his arms and shaking his head. He'd always believed that hiding in the shadows and living a quiet life was the best way to keep the peace for their sort, but watching the girls beam up at

JUST A LITTLE CHRISTMAS

the men of Darlington Gardens, as though they were gifts from God, made him wonder if the real key to acceptance lay with the younger generation. How different would all of their lives be if children were never taught to hate? If they were taught that everyone deserved respect, no matter how different they were. It seemed so possible within that brightly decorated ballroom, filled with song and friendship, but the real world was so different. The real world contained men like Ian Archibald, who would steal another man's child and make ridiculous demands just so he could enrich himself. It contained vicious lords who saw children as commodities, like the ones David and Lionel had fought so hard to take down over the summer.

He glanced across the audience to where David and Lionel sat next to the cluster of girls. Lionel had a mischievous look in his eyes and seemed to be whispering to Blake's daughters about something, but that wasn't what drew John's attention. Two rows behind David sat Detective Arthur Gleason. John's gut clenched and his blood pulsed faster, not only because Gleason was staring right at him with a sly grin, as if mocking John for only just noticing him now, but because Gleason was exactly the sort of man, like Ian Archibald and the villainous lords, who made the world a worse place for his presence in it. Or so John was convinced. He didn't have proof yet, but he was certain that Gleason was working for Ian Archibald, attempting to find a missing Egyptian medallion for him. A medallion that John needed to locate first

MERRY FARMER

so that he could use it as a bargaining chip in his efforts to get Blake's son back.

John glared at the detective, in spite of the cheerful crescendo of the song that filled the room as the panto came to a close. Rather than glare right back, Gleason winked at him and bit his lip. The overtly sexual look sent John's senses spinning, and he snapped his head forward to the stage again. He refused to let Gleason get the better of him, even if the man was as tempting as a treacle tart and would be twice as fun to devour. Their day would come, but not tonight.

The pantomime finished with the actors tossing handfuls of sweets and small toys to the girls in the audience. John's smile returned as he watched the delightful little creatures leap out of their chairs to gather up as many of the treats as they could. Most of them looked as though they'd never had anything half so wonderful happen to them in their lives. John's attention was drawn to the side of the room, where Martin Piper, dressed as Father Christmas, had gone to fetch a bulging sack of presents, but before he could come forward, Lionel leapt out of his seat and took to the stage.

"Ladies and gentlemen and those somewhere in between," he began, arms outstretched, earning a chuckle from the audience. "Before we move on to the wining and dining part of our evening, the girls have a surprise for you."

The sea of little girls scrambling for sweets stopped what they were doing and rushed to the stage, crowding

JUST A LITTLE CHRISTMAS

around Lionel. A few of the older girls who hadn't partic-
ipated in the dash for treats stepped forward from the
back of the room, carrying boxes that were overflowing
with bits of silver cloth and spangled stars. They
proceeded to hand what looked like angel costumes and
props to the other girls as they formed rows on the stage.

"The impish little minxes of Darlington Gardens
have a surprise for all of you, their fathers and uncles and
aunts and friends, who have done so much to care for
them and keep them safe this year," Lionel went on,
moving to the side so that the girls could take center
stage. "They have worked very hard indeed to prepare
this treat for you, and I'm sure you will enjoy it."

Lionel stepped off the stage as the audience
applauded. John found it touching that a passel of grown
men suddenly looked as rapt and excited as the girls had
before the panto started. David stood and nudged Blake
off of the piano bench, taking his place, then launched
into the opening bars of an old, familiar Christmas song.
Blake moved straight to Niall's side where he stood
against the wall, watching, and took his hand, leaning his
head against Niall's. As soon as the sound of nearly three
dozen, angelically sweet voices launched into the beautiful hymn and accompanying dance, John felt tears
stinging his eyes as his throat closed up. He laughed at
himself. He'd never considered himself a sentimental
fool, but there was something about the beauty and joy of
the moment, about the innocence of the girls and their
song, and the emotion that filled the room.

MERRY FARMER

Christmas truly was a magical time. For just one moment, there was peace on earth, even for men like them. They'd all come together as an extended family, without judgement or persecution. Out of the corner of his eye, John spotted dozens of men and women holding hands, leaning into each other, and wiping away sentimental tears. For just that moment, no one was out to destroy them or tell them they couldn't live or love the way they wanted to. Who knew what tomorrow would bring, but in that moment, they all knew they had each other. Even Gleason looked touched when John stole a glance at him. The man's eyes were glassy with sentiment, and when he peeked at John and their eyes met, Gleason's smile was genuine and warm. Perhaps he wasn't such a horrible—

His thought was cut short as the doors at the back of the ballroom clattered open and Danny Long marched into the room, eyes wide.

"Sorry, loves," he told the girls, who were just finishing the last verse of their song. His expression and tone of voice were grave as he glanced across the adults. "I hate to interrupt such a charming performance, but Officer Murdoch is back, and he's brought friends."

CHAPTER 10

A ripple of anxiety passed through the ballroom at Danny's announcement. Several men rose immediately from their seats, frowning, their jaws and fists clenched. More than a few others clasped their friends or lovers close, eyes wide with fear. They all knew that, as bad as it was that Officer Murdoch was back, the fact that he'd brought more officers with him meant only one thing—the raid on Darlington Gardens that they'd all feared so much could actually be happening.

"Do they know there's a party here this evening?" Max said, breaking away from where he'd been sitting with Stephen to watch the show. "Have they figured out most of the neighborhood is here?"

"I think so," Danny said, scrubbing a hand over his face. "I'm not letting any of them in, no matter what authority that prick Murdoch thinks he has." He glanced to the stage full of little girls dressed as angels. "Sorry," he

MERRY FARMER

apologized with a momentarily sly grin. He grew serious a second later. "I can send a runner to fetch Lord Clerkenwell, but—"

Before Danny could share his plan, the girls surprised everyone by surging off the stage and charging toward the back of the room.

"We're not having it," Katie shouted.

"For Darlington Gardens," Greta cried out, raising a fist in the air.

"Angels, wait! What in God's name are you doing?" Lionel yelped from the corner of the stage, then shot after them.

The stunned men watched in shock as the girls poured out of the ballroom, screaming and hollering as they went. As soon as they realized what was going on, they leapt into action, racing after them.

"Greta, Jessie, stop this instant," Blake shouted, shooting to the front of the pack, Niall right behind him.

"Did you have something to do with this?" David asked Lionel as they joined the chase.

"No!" Lionel insisted. "I have no idea what's going on. But I have to say, I'm impressed."

"I have a bad feeling about this," Stephen told Max as they pushed their way through the scrum at the door, then out into the hall and down the grand staircase in Danny and Phoebe's house to the front door.

By the time the first of the men made it into the street, the girls had already scattered into the lamp-lit darkness of

Darlington Gardens. Their silver angel costumes glinted in the gaslight as they dashed toward the corner of the park, the steps that led down to the kitchens in front of some of the townhouses, and the corners of buildings. Greta, Jessie, Jane, and Katie marched straight up to Officer Murdoch and the half dozen policemen who accompanied him. At least a dozen more officers were spread out up and down the streets of the square, staring at the cheerily-decorated houses and scratching their heads.

"Halt! Who goes there?" Jane shouted as she and the other three ringleaders reached Officer Murdoch. Jane held out her hands, as though she could stop them with that alone, as Greta, Jessie, and Katie all crossed their arms and stood like immovable pillars.

Officer Murdoch flinched at first, then rolled his shoulders and laughed at the girls, as though they were a joke. "Well don't you lot look pretty, all dressed up like angels," he told them in a sing-song voice.

The officers flanking him laughed with them. At least until the men from the party began to flood into the street behind them. Then they were immediately on their guard, pulling out their billy clubs and attempting to look fierce.

"How dare you invade our square?" Greta demanded, puffing up her chest.

One of the other girls who had dashed into the shadows around the square darted up to her, handing her a club of her own that had been carved from a thick

MERRY FARMER

branch. The same girl armed Jessie, Jane, and Katie as well.

"Well, love," Officer Murdoch continued, still using a treacly-sweet voice and bending over as if the girls needed him to address them at their level to be understood. "Seems there are some bad men who live in your square. Perverted men. Dangerous men. Me and my friends here have come to ferret them out and take them all to jail, understand?"

"By what right have you come to raid—"

David didn't get any further than that before Katie cried out, "This is *our* home, and they are *our* grown-ups! We don't want you here."

Officer Murdoch straightened, frowning in puzzlement at the resistance the girls presented. He narrowed his eyes at the increasing wall of men standing behind the girls—who now seemed to be spread out around the square, all of them looking menacing and holding what looked like sticks and sling-shots.

"You don't understand," Officer Murdoch said, the sweetness gone from his voice. "This place is a cesspool, and I don't care what orders came down from Lord Clerkenwell, we're here to clean house and—"

"Charge!"

Greta screamed the order before Officer Murdoch could finish. A swelling battle cry rang out all around the square. With it came a flurry of hurled pine cones and rocks aimed at the police officers. Officer Murdoch and his companions flinched and ducked under the initial

JUST A LITTLE CHRISTMAS

assault, too surprised to do anything but shield their faces.

The girls saw that as proof that they had all the power. They ran toward the officers, more than three dozen of them, flailing their sticks and screaming at the startled and terrified men like banshees. None of the girls were strong enough to cause more than bruises and an occasional cut, but the sheer terror they inspired by their ferocity had the hapless officers staggering backward, looking for cover.

"What are you little monsters doing?" Officer Murdoch yelped as Greta and Jane smacked his knees and backside with their sticks as he tried to scramble away. "I'm an officer of Her Majesty's police. I'm trying to help you."

"We don't want your help," Jane shouted, growling as she smacked his arse. "This is our home, and we don't want you here."

All around the square, similar scenes were playing out. The stunned police officers didn't know what could have gone so wrong so quickly. They dodged and ducked away from the bloodthirsty little girls, scrambling toward the square's exits. One or two raised his club to threaten the snarling imps, but they couldn't bring themselves to actually hit a child, especially a girl, especially one dressed as an angel. When one of them did strike out at Ursula, two of his fellow officers rounded on him and took him to task for it so viciously that it appeared as though those officers had joined the girls' cause.

MERRY FARMER

"Should we help them?" Everett asked from the crowd of men lining the street along the end of the square where Danny's house stood.

Patrick turned to them, arms crossed, a slight grin twitching on his mouth. "Do they look like they need help?"

"No," Everett admitted, laughing.

"Someone is going to get hurt," Stephen fretted. "We have to stop this."

"I agree," Blake said, full of fatherly concern, stepping from the curb into the street.

"What's going on here?" a new voice startled him enough that he paused and turned back.

A police officer that none of them had seen before strode in from the northwestern entrance to the square, a puzzled look on his face.

A fresh wave of concern passed through the men who stood watching the melee without knowing what to do.

"It's just a little Christmas pantomime," Lionel insisted, sweeping up to the man. He grabbed his arm and steered him to the side of the road opposite the men from the party so that he wouldn't be able to look too deeply into the crowd. "The girls are enacting, er...."

"The story of the angels leading the shepherds to Bethlehem to see our lord and savior's birth," David filled in, rushing up to the new officer's side to join Lionel.

"Yes, that's it," Lionel said, letting out a breath of relief.

The new officer glanced between the two of them,

JUST A LITTLE CHRISTMAS

then nodded toward the melee—which was moving farther and farther toward the other side of the square as the girls drove Officer Murdoch and his officers out the northeast entrance.

"They don't look like shepherds to me," the man said. "And if that's leading them to Bethlehem, then I'd hate to be among them."

"Yes, the girls are a bit exuberant, aren't they?" Lionel said with a laugh.

The new officer raised an eyebrow at him, as if he didn't believe a word Lionel was saying. He nodded at the pack of officers and girls again. "That Officer Richard Murdoch?" he asked.

"I, er, believe it is?" David answered nervously.

The new officer snorted. "Right prick, that one. He's never gonna hear the end of this. Getting beaten to a pulp by a pack of girls." The officer chuckled louder. "I can't wait to tell the rest of the lads about this." He thumped David on the shoulder, then sauntered down the street as if to catch up with Officer Murdoch and his crew. "You gents have a merry Christmas. Enjoy your fancy dress party."

The men who had watched the entire encounter with baited breath let out a collective sigh of relief.

"Do you think Murdoch is going to tell anyone about this and come after us for revenge?" James asked Samuel Percy, who'd ended up next to him.

Samuel laughed. "Not if he knows what's good for him."

"Not if it means confessing to being bested by a pack of wild girls," Martin laughed, still dressed as Father Christmas.

A cry of victory sounded from the other end of the square as the girls chased the last of the invading officers out of Darlington Gardens. They waved their clubs and slingshots in the air, hugging each other and jumping up and down.

"We did it!" Beatrice shouted. "We won, we actually won!"

Several of the girls burst into tears while others shrieked with laughter. After the horrible, miserable, sad year so many of them had had, they'd finally achieved something that made them feel powerful. They clustered together as they marched back across the square to where their grown-ups were watching outside of Mr. and Lady Long's house, bursting into song as they did. It wasn't the sweet Christmas carol they'd sung before, but rather a raunchy, ribald song that one of the older girls had taught them.

"Oh, dear," Max said, laughing even as he shook his head. "They're going to be impossible to handle after this."

"And they have every right to be," Stephen said with a proud smile, hugging Max from the side. "They've earned this. We've all earned this."

The victorious girls were greeted with open arms, hugs, and kisses from the men they were certain they'd saved. They all headed back into the big house, back to

JUST A LITTLE CHRISTMAS

the ballroom—which was decidedly warmer and cozier than the frosty night street. They were rewarded for their efforts with sweets and punch and more hugs as the gentlemen of Darlington Gardens marveled at their bravery and asked them how they'd planned the whole thing.

"Someone is going to have to contact Scotland Yard to explain," David murmured to John as the two of them stood off to the side of the room with Danny. "Even if Murdoch is too embarrassed by the whole thing to own up to what happened, if we want to stop holy hell from raining down on us as retaliation, someone is going to have to smooth things over."

"I'll take care of it," Danny said. "Jack already had plans to squelch Murdoch. But with any luck, this will send the message to anyone else foolish enough to set their sights on Darlington Gardens that the neighborhood is protected."

"I'll say it is," John laughed, shaking his head.

As far as the girls were concerned, they'd more than earned their presents from Father Christmas. As Martin gathered them all at the front of the room near the stage to hand out the brightly-wrapped gifts that the men of the square had put together for each of them, some of the girls recognized him as Mr. Piper. But most of the younger ones watched Father Christmas with wide eyes, believing that he hadn't forgotten them after all. He'd brought them presents, but more importantly, the grown-ups in their lives hadn't pushed them aside or bullied them or done horrible things to them. They had food, warm clothes, nice places to sleep, and friends like they'd never had before. They were safe, and as far as they were concerned—as far as the adults were concerned too—that was the best Christmas gift anyone could have given them.

So! I bet you're wondering...how historically accurate is it to have an entire square in London inhabited by gay men and their families? Actually, it's way more historically accurate than you might suspect! Yes, I've exaggerated Darlington Gardens to serve my purposes, but the geography of the square itself is based on one of my favorite places to stay in Earl's Court, Barkston Gardens. Look it up on a map and you'll see what I visualize Darlington Gardens to look like (minus one of the roads leading into the square).

But is it accurate to have an entire neighborhood of gay men?

Yep! In fact, London had several "gay-friendly" neighborhoods that dated back to the Middle Ages. Everything was, necessarily, top secret, but ironically, the existence of these enclaves and establishments and guides to finding them could be found in pornographic literature of the era, such as *Yokel's Preceptor, or More Sprees in London* (c1855) and *Sins of the Cities of the Plain* (1881), or in anti-gay tracts that supposedly repudiated homosex-

JUST A LITTLE CHRISTMAS

uality while inadvertently giving visitors to the city a list of places they could go to get a little action, such as *Tempted London* (1889) and *In The Year of Jubilee* (1894). Meanwhile, authors such as Oscar Wilde, John Addington Symonds, Roger Casement, George Ives, G.S. Street, and many others wrote thinly-veiled descriptions of familiar haunts and gay neighborhoods in their poetry and prose that anyone in the know would have recognized.

These hang-outs and neighborhoods were in constant danger of being raided by men like Officer Murdoch, based on information given to them by professional black-mailers. Yep, that's right, there were actually men and women in this era who made their living off of luring gay men into situations where they would be exposed, then collecting an under-the-table fee from corrupt policemen once the victims were arrested. But the safe places and communities did exist. We may never truly know how extensive these communities were, because the bulk of the historical records we have are a result of the men who were caught, not the ones who sailed peacefully under the radar. Just like the histories of people of color and of women, a lot of it has been swept under the carpet and is only now being rediscovered. Gay History is a relatively new field of study, with more and more information coming to light all the time.

· · ·

MERRY FARMER

ONE OTHER NOTE. THE CLEVELAND STREET scandal, which I mentioned in this story, was a very real event that had a profoundly negative impact on the lives of gay men in the 1890s. It involved the exposure of a brothel that specialized in *very* young men and boys. That was shocking enough, but when it was found that the patrons of this brothel were noblemen and other prominent members of high society, the public went nuts over it. And yes, it is highly likely that the Prince of Wales, the future Kind Edward VII, and members of the royal family patronized the place, but of course that was covered up. Not well enough for history to forget about it, though! I mentioned in this story that all it would take was one more high-profile case to destroy decades of hard-won obscurity and peace for gay men, and that case ended up being the trial of Oscar Wilde in 1895.

Once again, the public ate up every sordid detail of Oscar Wilde's life. Since the details sold papers and made a lot of people rich, the years after Wilde's trial were filled with danger for the gay community as unscrupulous blackmailers left no stone unturned looking for the next headline-grabbing arrests. Unfortunately for your average gay man, the actions of a few made life way more difficult for everyone else. After what had been a decades-long period of relative peace and obscurity for the gay community, the 1890s saw an increase in persecution and arrests for gross indecency that lasted until the end of the First World War...when

JUST A LITTLE CHRISTMAS

everyone's morals loosened up a little. But the 1920s is a whole other story!

THE BROTHERHOOD SERIES DOESN'T END HERE! THE next book in the series, *Just a Little Madness*, comes next! When extroverted and sexually liberated actor, Martin Piper, and straight-laced, repressed politician, Edward Archibald, team up to hunt down Edward's brother Ian, the chemistry and chaos might just drive them mad!

IF YOU ENJOYED THIS BOOK AND WOULD LIKE TO HEAR more from me, please sign up for my newsletter! When you sign up, you'll get a free, full-length novella, *A Passionate Deception*. Victorian identity theft has never been so exciting in this story of hope, tricks, and starting over. Part of my West Meets East series, *A Passionate Deception* can be read as a stand-alone. Pick up your free copy today by signing up to receive my newsletter (which I only send out when I have a new release)!

Sign up here: http://eepurl.com/cbaVMH

ARE YOU ON SOCIAL MEDIA? I AM! COME AND JOIN the fun on Facebook: http://www.facebook.com/merryfarmerreaders

. . .

MERRY FARMER

I'M ALSO A HUGE FAN OF INSTAGRAM AND POST LOTS of original content there: https://www.instagram.com/merryfarmer/

Click here for a complete list of other works by Merry Farmer.

ABOUT THE AUTHOR

I hope you have enjoyed *Just a Little Christmas*. If you'd like to be the first to learn about when new books in the series come out and more, please sign up for my newsletter here: http://eepurl.com/cbaVMH And remember, Read it, Review it, Share it! For a complete list of works by Merry Farmer with links, please visit http://wp.me/P5ttjb-14F.

Merry Farmer is an award-winning novelist who lives in suburban Philadelphia with her cats, Torpedo, her grumpy old man, and Justine, her hyperactive new baby. She has been writing since she was ten years old and realized one day that she didn't have to wait for the teacher to assign a creative writing project to write something. It was the best day of her life. She then went on to earn not one but two degrees in History so that she would always have something to write about. Her books have reached the Top 100 at Amazon, iBooks, and Barnes & Noble, and have been named finalists in the prestigious RONE and Rom Com Reader's Crown awards.

ACKNOWLEDGMENTS

I owe a huge debt of gratitude to my awesome beta-readers, Caroline Lee, Laura Stapleton, and Jolene Stewart, for their suggestions and advice. Double thanks to Julie Tague, for being a truly excellent editor. And a great big thanks to my assistant, Cindy Jackson!

Click here for a complete list of other works by Merry Farmer.

Printed in Great Britain
by Amazon